EMBRACE OF THE SANDMAN

DEATH IS NOT THE END

ELLIS LEIGH

kinship press

EMBRACE OF THE SANDMAN

My death wasn't right.

It wasn't fair or just. My murder was a punishment I hadn't deserved, and killing me affected my fated mate much worse than anyone could have expected. I am allowed to continue in the land of the dead, not living but not gone, while he lives a half-life. A lonely one, empty of love. I see him. I watch him. I know he misses me every day.

I miss him too.

So much.

Enough to defy Death himself...and find a way to reunite with my mate.

His friends call him Sandman. I call him mine.

CHAPTER 1

THE GLIMPSE

One lesson I had learned since being murdered was that Death was not a beast to be trifled with. The being always had been and always would be sitting between the land of the living and the various afterlives afforded to those who made it past him. And most made it past him. He wasn't an evil overlord or some sort of demon devouring every being he came across. Death didn't steal souls; he simply took advantage of those who became confused along the way. Who perhaps weren't quite ready to say goodbye and lingered a bit too long on his turf. He was far more opportunistic than evil.

Though, occasionally he made an example of the ones he felt deserved the nothingness—the utter and total finality—his appetite afforded them.

Death primarily fed himself on convenience, assisted by the creatures he worked with—the Grim Reaper, Hypnos, and the Keres sisters. I had been assigned the position of Keres when I'd passed over, lingering far too long in the land between. Death had apparently seen something in my soul that better served him than fed him. I had done my duty with him for a century and a half, bringing him lost souls and those refusing to move into the afterlife. Corralling the ones who deserved a true ending. I had fed the beast well.

But even a Keres sister needed a break.

My paws slammed onto the trail through the woods, my claws digging into the dirt with each landing. Propelling my body forward as the wolf who lived inside me followed the pull only she could feel. The one taking us to where we wanted to be. Or at least, as far as I could go without figuring out a way to cross back over into the living realm. Into the world I still missed every single day. The one so very different from where I now resided.

The forests in the land of the dead were nothing like the ones I had lived my life in. The only similarities were tall trees and soft ground beneath my paws as I ran. The old woods—the ones from when I had been alive—had been filled with sounds of life and colors so vibrant, a single patch of flowers could have distracted me for hours. The woods I had run thorough since my death were all gray and dull, the colors flat or lacking. The scents rising from the earth filled with rot and decay instead of life. Everything dead. Everything empty.

The Grim Reaper's lover had called this place the Reversed because of how the colors seemed backward. How the sky glowed but in an odd, dark sort of way. How the smoke rose from the living things as if Death himself were slowly tearing us apart. A fitting description and a likely possibility.

But one of the things about the Reversed that worked in my favor was the ability to see what the living were up to. Not all of them—not even most of them. We waited to be called on to deal with souls trapped between the living and the afterlife, so it wasn't as if visages of the living going about their daily tasks filled the Reversed. If you truly wanted to see someone, if there was a living person you had a connection to, you could watch them, though. If you knew where they were in the living realm, you could see.

Thankfully, I knew where the person I wanted to check in on resided.

It didn't take more than half a day for me to arrive at the proper location, to be pulled by Fate to where my soul felt she was needed. Still in wolf form, I slowed to a walk and then a predator's creep as I grew closer to my quarry. As I tried and failed to place the sounds coming from up ahead. Whoosh-thwak. Whoosh-thwak. The strange noises were strong and loud, obviously coming from outside of any structure that would have muffled them. That meant my target would be out in the open. Ready to be seen. Soon. Just a few more steps. I trembled with anticipation, wanting so much to run and jump at him. To announce my presence and see the man smile my way. To feel the joy of reuniting with him.

Impossible, but I couldn't stop the desire from building.

I crept from around a stand of trees and nearly whimpered at the sight before me. The man I had been seeking, the one I had run such a long distance for, stood outside a small, boxy house with an ax in his hands. That had been the sound—the whoosh of the ax swinging through the air and the thwack of it hitting the chunks of wood he had been splitting. He stood in all his glory, shirtless and strong as ever, chopping pieces of wood smaller and smaller.

Memories slammed into me as I watched him, moments from my time in the living realm I usually kept locked away because they hurt too much to think about while living my non-life. That same man as a boy, running through the woods with me. Swimming in the river that ran through the parklands. Both of us young and silly and such good friends. He'd taught me how to survive the wilderness on our first camping trip together, had helped the younger humans in our group learn the importance of fire when living in the wild. I remembered the beginning of our lives together, and while the pain of all I had lost still came, the memories seemed worth it with him so close to me. They seemed necessary.

I settled in to watch and let my mind wander back to the before. To first hand-holding moments and stolen kisses. To hours spent under the sun in fields of wild flowers. To the happiness and comfort only he could have provided me. To the joy I had once known.

Whether minutes or hours later, not long after the man had headed inside the little house, the sound of a car pulling up drew my attention and brought me back to the present. Such an odd thing to hear—I hadn't seen a vehicle that wasn't about to crash since I'd died and ended up in this realm. But the car didn't crash. It came rolling to a stop on the driveway instead. My vision into the living realm seemed clearer than usual, so I paid attention. I even slunk closer, unable to ease my curiosity, a feeling of familiarity making my instincts slip into defensive mode. Two people stepped out of the vehicle as I watched, a man and a woman. Both unremarkable and yet worrisome. I watched as they climbed the porch steps and walked to the door. As they knocked. As the door swung inward and the man I'd come to see appeared.

The vision of him—no shirt, jeans slung low on his hips, barefoot—caused more memories to infiltrate my mind. Clips of the two of us together with him dressed like that. Of how warm all that exposed skin would be. Of how he would tug me into his arms and—

I whimpered, but thankfully, no one else heard the pitiful sound.

"Corbinan," the woman said, addressing the man in the door. My hackles rose, both at how familiar she seemed to me even though I couldn't remember from where, and at the use of his full name. He didn't like people calling him that. Never had. He much preferred his nickname. "It's so good to see you."

The man—Corbin—crossed one ankle over the other and leaned a shoulder against the doorframe, blocking their entrance. The epitome of nonchalant.

"You're wasting your time."

His tone sent a chill up my spine, the venom dripping from every word sparking something inside my mind. Something forgotten but dangerous. I inched closer. Needing to see. Wishing so much to run up onto that porch and stand between them.

The woman smiled, the expression turning my stomach and stoking a rage within me that I remembered but couldn't place the root cause of. I had been gone too long, had been in the realm of the dead for too many years to count. My memories of my life before—of anything not having to do with Corbin—had eroded. I didn't remember her, but I knew she did not have good intentions.

"We want you to come home," she said, a fake, overly sweet tone in her voice that had me on high alert. Had me concerned for Corbin's well-being. "It's been so long—"

"One hundred forty-seven years, eight months, and twelve days."

The woman jerked back, her smile falling. "What?"

"You said it's been so long. I assume you meant since you killed my mate. That was a mere one hundred forty-seven years, eight months, and twelve days ago. Or are we talking about something else?"

More memories, ones I'd tucked deep down in my mind, flooded back. The pack, the day Corbin was forced to fight for me, the five women showing up to our little cabin in the woods. The pain that came as four of them piled on me. I had been dead a long time and had taken joy in watching the end of those four women's lives over the years. I had stood back and allowed my Keres sister to exact my revenge one by one so they would never find their peace in the afterlife.

The last one stood at the door not twenty feet away from me. The fifth woman who had come to enact my death on that day so very long ago. The ringleader. Memories bubbled up, becoming more solid. Twisting my gut and filling my empty form with rage. She had been the pack Alpha's chosen mate, not fated like Corbin and I had been. When the Alpha had put a claim on me— had told Corbin he had a right and a responsibility to take me to his bed—my sweet man had fought for me. Her jealousy had boiled over, and while Corbin had been defending me, she'd come to take me out of the equation to keep her position of power.

I remembered.

And I was ready for her to die for what she had done.

Without thought or planning, I rushed forward, teeth bared and growl rumbling through the quiet woods. I jumped over the railing and landed a mere two feet away from my quarry. I didn't stop, though. I let my momentum push me up and forward, reaching high. One leap, opening my mouth to take her head with me. One bite was all it would take, so I slammed my jaws closed...

But I didn't connect with my prey.

I blasted right through her form, gaining not a single response from any of the living people on the porch as I twisted in midair and fell to the ground. Instead of ending up on the other side of them, though, I found myself in what looked like a cave. No house, no porch, no people—just a new place that was dark, damp, and awful. I swung around, still growling, trying to regain my bearings. To figure out what had just happened and how I had been transported to such a place.

The answer came with a chuckle, Death's own Hypnos practically being birthed by the shadows. Fitting for such a dark being.

"You know that's not allowed."

Such an arrogant bastard. I shifted to my human form, thankful in the afterlife that my shroud came with me so I did not have to stand naked before him.

"She deserves to die."

"Your sister is gone, so if you want that woman dead, you're going to have to do the dirty work. The right way—you can't kill her like you would have in the living world."

Guilt, heavy and dark, landed on my shoulders, and my stomach turned at the very idea of what I would have to do to seek my revenge. At the idea of stealing a soul from the living realm that wasn't ready to cross over. It wasn't something I had ever done. I collected and moved souls; I didn't snatch them.

"I don't think I can."

Hypnos huffed an irritated sound. "You and Grim—both so weak. Our job is to kill—"

"Our job is to assist people moving from the plane of the living to that of the dead."

"And occasionally devour their souls to feed our own." He stepped closer, crowding me, lowering his voice but making sure I heard him loud and clear. "You may have always seen yourself as above the other Keres sister because she was so much more violent and aggressive with her feeding, but you do the same thing."

"I don't enjoy it."

"But you still do it." He took a step back and sighed,

picking at his nails as if bored. "Tell you what. I'll help you if you help me."

"What do you mean?"

"I'll take care of the woman for you—you help me figure out how to kill my witch so she can join me here."

His witch. The one from Mackinac Island. The young woman he had become obsessed with. The one related to Grim's dead witch lover.

Hypnos was playing a dangerous game with that one.

"I won't kill for you," I said, knowing nothing good would come from going up against witches. Especially not Grim's witch and her family. Those were powerful beings.

Hypnos didn't like my response. "Then I guess you're on your own. But know that I'll be watching you."

With a flick of his wrist, I went tumbling backward through a darkness I had never experienced before. Within seconds, I had landed almost right back where I'd started. I spilled out of Hypnos's weird time and space tunnel onto the grass in front of the house. The daylight no longer brightened the forest, night and shadows reigning instead. I looked around, breathing hard as the reality that Hypnos had somehow moved me to a different realm within the land of the dead making my head spin, the changes around me not helping matters.

Everything looked different.

I saw no sign of the woman, no sign of my mate

either. The house wasn't silent as if he had retired to sleep, though. It sat empty and almost...dead. All signs of life had been whisked away. There was no ax, no pile of logs, and no remnants of sawdust near Corbin's wood-cutting stump. No cars in the driveway, no lights on inside. I had no idea what day it was, how many hours or weeks I'd spent in that little hellscape with Hypnos, but understanding the passing of time would not change the end result. My mate had disappeared.

CHAPTER 2
THE THREAT

While time in the land of the dead passed much differently than it did in the living realm, it still mattered. Still carried a weight and a sense of importance as it flowed around us. It took me an exorbitant amount of time to find Corbin after I'd lost him at the forest house. Far too many days and nights spent hunting my realm for signs of him, howling up to the moon to ask for her assistance.

Once again, the fated connection between Corbin and me directed me westward across the United States, leading me by our bond until I made it to a little valley in the Carson Range just outside of Reno, Nevada. Why Corbin had chosen the region, I had no idea, but from the first moment I once again laid eyes on him, from the second I saw the little log cabin in the woods so much like the one we had lived in before my death, I felt at home.

The man had found a place to stay that reminded him of our life together.

I couldn't stay all the time—I did have work to do for Death—but I enjoyed my time curled up in the woods. Spent as much time as possible keeping watch over him. Observing Corbin living his life was something I did well. Whenever I found myself near Reno, I kept my eyes on him and his home in the forest. And while I watched, I did my best not to whimper or cry. Oh, how I missed him. But his life seemed comfortable, almost joyous at times. He deserved that.

Watching him also made me realize just how much he'd grown since my death. He was so much more adult. Even with seventy years under our belts as a mated couple before my murder, we had still been kids in a lot of ways. He wasn't a kid anymore. Corbin carried an air about him, one of danger. Of power. He rode a motorcycle around town—something he'd started after my death— which only fed into that sense of danger. Only amplified the *grown man* aspects of him. The *don't fuck with me* vibe he gave off.

All signs of the youthful boy with the sweet smile who had brought me wild flowers every week just to see my eyes light up were gone. I missed him, but I had to admit, this rougher, tougher version of Corbin appealed.

After a particularly gruesome and long soul retrieval for Death that had taken me halfway around the world, I hurried back to the small pocket of happiness outside Reno. Lost in my memories of my life before, I crested a hilltop and spotted the little cabin and the man I couldn't seem to move on from sitting outside. I nearly sighed at the vision, knowing he'd remained safe while I'd handled business for Death. He'd lived his life while I'd been sent to do the job that kept me living this odd non-life. That kept him in my world.

Corbin sat on the porch as the sky went gloomy, as the living world began to prepare for their hours of rest. He had his feet up on the railing, had a glass of something golden brown at his fingertips. He looked comfortable and calm and altogether peaceful. I envied him that.

"You shouldn't be here."

I jerked and growled, quieting as I spotted Grim not ten feet away from me. The big, scarred almost-demon leaned nonchalantly against the trunk of a tree as if he'd been there for hours. Ankles crossed and body barely more than shadows. Sneaky, sneaky.

I shifted forms, my wolf tucked away but not hidden, ending on two feet instead of four. I crossed my arms and stood tall. Ready to fight if necessary. "Why not?"

He nodded toward Corbin, his black eyes never leaving mine. "Do I really need to answer that?"

"Yeah, you do. Because if you're implying I can't

spend my downtime watching the man the Fates tied my soul to at birth, we're going to need to have a conversation about hypocrisy."

"It's not the same."

That comment, the disregard for my mating bond, considering his situation, made my temper burn bright and hot. The men in the land of the undead were very good at stomping on my last nerve.

"Yes, it is," I said, storming closer. "If I shouldn't be here, then perhaps you shouldn't spend so much time focused only on the door into the Summerlands."

"My witch is there."

"And my mate is here."

"But he's not dead, is he?"

And that fact...there was no arguing with it.

Grim eventually sighed. "It's for his sake as much as yours, Margaret."

I had no words of response for that statement, so I held my tongue. We sat in silence as the sun set, as the shadows around us grew deeper. As the living world began to move toward their hours of sleep. I held my tongue the entire time, keeping my eyes on Corbin. Refusing to look away, even for a moment. Refusing to accept the truth Grim had laid bare for me.

Eventually, though, I broke. "How do you do it?"

Grim didn't need more than my quiet question to understand the path of my thoughts.

"It's a struggle, but she's worth it."

"I don't want him to die."

"I can see that."

I turned, facing the creature who had always been reasonable with me. Perhaps not always kind, but level-headed. Something I needed right then.

"What do I do?"

Before Grim could answer, the wind picked up, a cold blast of air disrupting the peace and the quiet that had settled around us. It was far too late for the zephyr to storm through. That, tied with a sense of the blast being unnatural and filled with negativity, sent my instincts into high gear. Grim and I jumped to our feet just as Hypnos appeared. The bastard looked almost gleeful. That was a bad sign.

"I did you a favor, Peggy."

By the Fates, I hated when he called me that. I also hated when he claimed to have done me a favor. Hypnos didn't understand the meaning of the word. To him, all favors—including ones the gifted didn't ask for—came with a cost. One he set and didn't inform you of until after. Being indebted to such a creature was a bad idea from the jump.

"I didn't ask you to do anything," I said, keeping my voice calm and flat. Not giving him an inch.

"I know, but it seemed needed." He shrugged a single shoulder, a casual move for a not-casual beast. "See, you've been without a sister for too long, and your work has been suffering because of it. This last retrieval at the internment camp—you could have brought Death so many more souls had you traveled with a second Keres. I mentioned that to Death, and he agreed that a single Keres wasn't enough to contain all the souls traipsing through his land to their afterlives."

I glanced at Grim, who looked almost as worried as I felt, my stomach sinking at the realization of what was coming. "What did you do?"

"Death and I made you a new sister." Hypnos waved an arm, and a cloud of smoke appeared, screaming into the quiet and racing through the air. Once it had completed the show, it landed and solidified, taking on a human shape. A female shape. One I knew.

One I recognized.

"Margaret? Is that you?" the dead woman asked, watching me as I tried to make sense of the vision before me. Her wicked chuckle didn't help my sense of confusion and rage. "I can't say I expected to see you here."

"What did you do, Hypnos?" Grim asked, but I already knew. I had already pinpointed my mistake. I'd been enraged when she'd shown up at Corbin's last home, had shown my hand by attempting to attack her. Hypnos had been there, had seen, and he'd chosen to take the opportunity to torture me just a little more than usual. To twist the knife already embedded deep in my flesh.

I didn't need him to tell me what he'd done because the woman who'd planned my murder was standing right there before me. My new so-called *sister*.

Still, Hypnos laughed, turning his attention to Grim. "I gave our Peggy a gift she needed and wanted. That's all."

The woman—her name escaping my memories as it always did—looked right over my shoulder, her smile widening. Her teeth bared and dripping the thick black ooze that appeared when our hunger for souls struck.

"Oh, I remember him."

Hypnos leaned over her shoulder to whisper in her ear, though he kept his eyes on mine and his voice loud enough for all of us to hear. "He could be your first."

"No," I spat, coming to rest not two feet before the couple without even having made the decision to move. "That's not happening."

The woman stared me down, a haughty expression on her face as she asked, "Says who?"

"Says me."

She leaned closer, stopping with our noses barely an inch apart. "If I remember right, you lost last time, pup."

The pop of the Ps in pup sent black ooze shooting from her mouth. I wiped the splatter off my face, keeping my glare locked on her. Not backing down for a second.

Yes, I'd lost last time I'd faced off with her. But I wasn't the same young shifter who had put faith in her packmates and the rules they lived under. I wasn't the girl who trusted easily anymore. And I wasn't a woman who would bow down to a bully.

"I did lose last time. But you don't have four lackeys to do your dirty work this time, bitch. It's one-on-one, and I know you can't take me."

The woman took a step back, her expression wavering but not breaking. Reality settling in through her anger. She may have been a Keres sister, but she was new to the world. New to the powers. She didn't have the control or stamina of someone with my level of experience. Thankfully for her, she seemed to grasp that knowledge just in time.

One last look over my shoulder gave away her true desires, though. "Perhaps another time for him."

"Perhaps you should try me and find out just how dangerous I've become."

She chuckled softly, smirking as she looked me up and down. "Perhaps I will."

Hypnos chuckled, obviously enjoying the tension between us. I glared in his direction, not allowing the woman to move out of my sight line.

"You have made a terrible mistake with this one, Hypnos."

He shrugged, irritatingly apathetic. "I don't think I

have, but I guess time will tell. Come, Kapila. We have souls to feed to Death."

Kapila. The chosen mate of my former pack's Alpha. The woman who had plotted and carried out my death. I wouldn't forget her name again; that was for sure.

Without another word, Kapila grabbed Hypnos by the arm, and the two dissolved into smoke, rising across the forest and disappearing into the night sky. I stood for a long moment, Grim at my side. Neither of us speaking as the gravity of what had just happened settled over me.

He broke the silence first that time. "What are you going to do?"

I looked out across the forest to the little cabin now glowing with a light that looked completely out of place in the cold, gray realm of death. The Reversed. But not everything seemed backward here. That woman, that threat, were all very real, just as they'd been when I'd been alive. I hadn't heeded the warnings then.

I had learned my lesson.

"I'm going to keep him alive. No matter what."

CHAPTER 3
THE TEAR

I ended up spending all my time watching over Corbin. Every day and night, I stayed in those woods, keeping an eye on that cabin, and learning so much new information about the man I'd once known everything about. About the man I'd spent seventy years with before he had been stolen away from me. I learned about his quietness and his love for a solitary life, both rather surprising, considering the memories of him from our pack days.

I also learned he had a number of friends whom he showed honest affection for. His weird little wireless phone rang every day, one of the men from his motorcycle club on the other end of the call. They called him Sandman and made him smile. His voice sounded almost chipper as he chatted with people I had never met but whom he obviously cared about. He'd ask about their mates and their children, would check in on how the big boss was doing—I had no idea who that was, but apparently he had *two* mates and was doing well—and would spend a portion of his day connecting with others.

Every day they called, and every day he perked up and chatted for a good hour or more with someone. But every day, after the call, he went right back to his quiet, calm self. Contemplative was a word I would have used for what Corbin had become. He stared off into the woods a lot, looking very much like a man lost in his thoughts. Not unhappy in appearance, but alone. Comfortable and solitary but loved—I would have enjoyed living that life with him. Would have liked to have added a little companionship into his world.

Grim visited me in those woods quite often. Not as regular as the phone calls Corbin received, but close. Grim would sit in silence with me. Or sometimes not silence.

"How is your mate?" Grim would occasionally ask.

My answer never changed. "Quiet but content. How is your witch?"

He liked talking about Amber, the dead witch who crossed afterlife planes to spend time with him. I had no idea how their relationship could work, no clue what happened when you fell in love while already dead, but they seemed to be making it work. I could hear it in

Grim's voice whenever he began to speak of her, could feel his energy shift. The man loved her and truly enjoyed his time with her. I felt conflicted about that, though. On the one hand, I was happy for Grim. He had found the person who spoke to his soul, and they truly enjoyed spending their time together. On the other, I had not been able to speak to my mate or hear him say my name in over a century. The bitterness of that truth stung, but I did my best to lock my sour grapes into a hiding spot in my mind. Still, whenever Grim would grow sad or say something about not spending enough time with her, I would remind him of what he truly had. I would tell him that at least he hadn't been stolen away from her to live a thousand lives in the hell we inhabited for no good reason. At least he had the little time with her that they managed to carve out.

But those grapes...they really were quite sour.

So, I sat, and I watched from deep within the trees, staying hidden even though there was no way Corbin could see me. Tucking myself into the shadows to exist alongside him. I hid just outside his space... Except for one night, when I felt particularly lonely. That night, the draw to him had crawled its way up my gullet and into my throat. The burn of need making it impossible to stand still. Impossible to resist. So I stopped trying.

Corbin had been outside all day, chopping wood and working on a small patch of ground at the back of the cabin that would have made a wonderful kitchen garden. I'd been too tired to resist the lure, too lonely and missing him too much to ignore the pang in my chest at the very sight of him. So once night began to fall, I crept closer. Inching my way into his space.

"Just a little bit," I said, convincing no one—not even myself—that I had any control over what I was about to do. "Not too much. I don't want to scare him."

As I lost my hold on the last thread of my self-control —and apparently my sanity, seeing as how talking to myself in the woods was likely a good indicator of *that*—I moved out of the tree line and into the open area at the edge of the property. The sun sat heavy and full in the western sky, the very top barely hanging on over the farthest treetops. The gloaming hour had come, my favorite time of the day when I'd been alive. I had always adored the deep orange and golden light that would pour down on us as the sun tucked itself away for the night, loved that single hour of deep blue shadows falling before the world went dark. Corbin and I had often sat outside together during that time, breathing in the last of the day. Stripping each other for shared intimate moments under the sky. He'd always looked amazing in that light. So alive.

Seeing him in his gray form, with no real color and looking washed out by the veil of death around me, made the constant missing of him so much worse. Made the memories hurt in new and deep ways. I existed in a state of emotional pain, but the sight of him made it worse. Made it pound harder than ever before. Being near him *hurt*, but I couldn't walk away.

As I stood closer than I should have been, staring across the clearing at the man himself as he grilled on the deck, I found myself truly missing everything about my life before. Colors, scents, the feel of fresh grass beneath my feet...all of it. But more than anything, I missed Corbin. I would have done anything for more time with him. Would have sold my soul again for a handful of minutes in his arms.

My left cheek suddenly grew wet, the hot liquid trailing down from my eye surprising me. I didn't cry— didn't allow the viscous black substance that served as the sole source of moisture within my body to escape. I'd refused to once I'd realized that crying no longer resulted in the tears of the living realm, but in that moment, my emotions grew so strong and powerful they were impossible for me to control. I cried. And I stood with what were likely tracks of black running down my face and over my jaw because they felt needed. Necessary.

One tear made it all the way down and escaped, a single drop of my pain falling from the edge of my jaw to the earth below. I looked down to watch as it dropped, almost witnessing the moment in slow motion. Amazed at how transparent that single tear appeared. Clear instead of black. Liquid instead of viscous. Almost like a real tear from a living being instead of whatever flowed inside my dead body.

I obsessed over watching the trajectory of that single drop. A tear falling should not have been so important. But this one felt different. Seemed vital.

That tear hit the earth without a sound, and yet as it landed, a deep rumble began right below my feet. A sound that caused the world to vibrate as it grew. That tremor spread out in a circle from the point of landing, a visual cue of something big and powerful happening. Something terrifying and new. As the tremble moved farther into the forest surrounding me, the light shifted. The colors growing deeper, brighter, more vibrant. I stood transfixed as the entire scene came to life before me, as if I had somehow cried my way back to the land of the living with its bright colors and vibrant foliage. An impossibility, and yet...

"Green," I said, picking up a fallen leaf and gawking at the richness of color in my hand. At how the deep shade contrasted with the pale peachiness of my skin. "How could I not remember..."

I looked up, needing to see more. Wanting to devour this moment and refill my memory banks. I'd forgotten how green the forest was and had misplaced the memory of the deep-blue tinge to the shadows as night fell. Had missed the scents that now filled my world—pine and water and dirt and all the things I had misplaced the names of. But the biggest shock, the most surprising in-full-color moment, came when I focused in on Corbin himself.

Oh, the man was still so beautiful.

His hair—a dirty-blond color—caught the light, hints of orange and red burning through the strands. It looked longer than I remembered him wearing it, but the need to run my fingers through it felt just as strong as when I'd been alive. I nearly whimpered as I fought to hold myself back. Instead of moving closer, I stood and stared, enraptured, taking in every detail. The golden tone of his skin. The faded blue of his pants, the dark shadows on his feet from walking around barefoot so much. Everything about him screamed man and strong and virile. And when he moved, when he stepped out from behind the grill so I could see all his inches, I nearly crumpled.

The man could not have been more gorgeous. My handsome, shirtless mate. The other half to my soul. By the Fates, how I had missed him.

But Corbin didn't stand still like a statue. No, he moved, flexing and stretching unconsciously as he flowed from one position to the next. I gasped, bringing my hand to my mouth as he turned and I got the view of his bare back. As I saw the muscles bunch and release, all that smooth skin covering them. It was an instinctual sound, one I couldn't hold back. One that shouldn't have been anything more than a whisper in the realm of the dead.

One he somehow heard...and reacted to.

Corbin turned and looked up, tantalizing blue eyes meeting mine for the first time in over a century. So deep in color, so filled with emotions I couldn't even name. He looked at me as if he could actually see me, as if he knew I was there, as if—

"Margaret?"

The pain of that word on his lips, the twisting of the knife of knowing he remembered me, dug deep into my soul. I let out a sob, overwhelmed with the feelings rushing through me. Unable to comprehend the what and how of the moment. Corbin took a step closer, his expression filled with shock, but it was too much. All too much. Instead of mirroring him to close the gap between us, I spun and ran into the woods. Shifted to my wolf form and dove deep into the grayness of my world. I couldn't stay, couldn't witness him turning colorless once more. Couldn't witness the pain of knowing I would never see him so bright and beautiful again.

I couldn't risk wanting to drag him into the afterlife with me to live out a half-existence devouring souls and shuttling the dead to whatever their fate happened to be.

But that moment, that beautiful connection of riotous color and endless emotion, would not be forgotten. That was not a memory I would tuck away and allow to fade. I would forever remember my mate standing there in all his glory, filled with color and life.

I would forever miss that version of Corbin more than any other.

The one I had never truly met.

The one I coveted more than anything else.

CHAPTER 4
THE FEAR

I didn't return to the cabin for days after the crying incident. Didn't seek out my mate in any way. Instead, I sulked along the edge of a big lake not too far from Corbin's place. I spent all my hours frozen in place, overwhelmed by emotions I hadn't been prepared to remember. Watching the water roll in and out along the shore and seeking some sort of connection to the world around me. There was none. Never had been. Not until the moment that tear had touched the ground. The moment I had somehow broken through the barrier between the living and the dead and I'd—

"Stop it," I hissed, still talking to myself. Still trying to make sense of everything that had happened without drowning in grief. "Just stop it already."

"Perhaps you should tell me what needs to be

stopped so I can offer my assistance." Grim appeared and sat down beside me, an action that did not take me by surprise. I had grown accustomed to his big, angry form showing up in unexpected places. The man had become my sidekick for some reason, appearing out of nowhere to offer some sort of comfort just when I felt everything slipping away from me. Just when it seemed I needed a friend the most. Not that he was my friend. But if he had been…

"I'm not in the mood to chat today." I pulled my knees up and rested my chin on them, keeping my focus on the trees across the lake. Keeping the brokenness inside me held together. "You might as well go."

"Not happening. You should really stop being so miserable."

I huffed, the sound coming out more like a snort than anything. "Oh sure, let me just get right on that."

"Is this because of what happened on Mackinac? Did you seeing people who knew him…break something?"

I sighed. The Mackinac fight—the battle to save his witch's sister from my former Keres sister—hadn't been the catalyst. I had been tracking and watching Corbin long before that, though less obsessively. No, the fight, seeing people I knew had connections to my mate, being seen by a living person who could bring him a message— all of that had made the wound of my loss deeper, but the wound had always been there. Festering just under the surface.

"It didn't break anything. The break has always been there."

Grim grunted his approval, seemingly not convinced. Not pushing me for more either. We ended up sitting in silence, his big, dark presence oddly comforting. I never would have called us friends—I didn't think I even understood what friends meant anymore, and he likely never had—but he'd always shown up when I needed him. He'd also sort of supported me when I'd gone against the whole "Keres sister" role, a fact I attributed to his independence and stubbornness. He rarely listened to what other people desired, as he usually demanded they do what he wanted. He was an okay guy, though, and I was out of options.

"I'm sad," I said, knowing that would grab his attention.

Instead of his usual grunt or know-it-all reply, he asked a simple, "Why?"

And *that* truly was the question of the day. I gave my answer a lot of thought, dug deep within myself to figure out why Corbin brought me sadness after over a century apart. It didn't take long to come up with an answer.

"Because I miss him. We were together a long time and were supposed to get forever, but the Fates and a group of jealous women ended that possibility when they ended my life." I looked off across the lake, taking a deep breath and truly giving myself over to the feelings being close to Corbin sparked. "I miss being able to talk to him and receive a hug from him and just *feel* him. You know?"

Grim gave me the grunt I had been expecting, an approving sort of sound that likely meant, yes, he did understand what I meant. The man had a woman he loved who was kept away from him, too.

"There has to be a way," he said.

I turned, my expression pulling tight across my forehead. "A way to what?"

"To spend time together. Actually together."

It was my turn to grunt. "The only *way* is for him to die, and that's not happening."

"What if it did?"

My growl came naturally, instinctually. My inner wolf responding to a threat to her mate. "Excuse me?"

Grim didn't flinch at the rumble directed at him. "He dies. Is that the worst thing you can imagine? We could handle his transition and lead his soul together—he could end up here with you. Would that really be so bad?"

"Hypnos and Kapila would devour his soul for Death to get back at me, leaving him without the afterlife he deserves. And I—"

"You would truly be alone," Grim said, settling deeper against a tree. "You and I are in the same boat."

"It's not a boat. It's a ship. And it's not just any ship. It's the *Titanic*."

"Don't remind me."

Well, that answer was unexpected and not able to be ignored. "You were at the sinking?"

Grim nodded slowly, still looking off into the forest. "Hypnos and your former sister had a blast that night."

"Seems fitting."

"They like the chaos, the aggressiveness of so many deaths at once. Battlegrounds are their favorite, but a solid passenger vessel sinking or airplane crash is a close second in their minds. The *Titanic* sinking so slowly brought the best of both to them."

"Were."

"What?"

I shrugged. "You said battlegrounds are their favorite. Were. She's dead. Your witch took care of that."

His face froze for a tiny second, all hard lines and jagged angles, then his lips alone began to rise in an evil-looking smile. "She did, didn't she?"

"You're so proud of that," I said, chuckling. Unable not to give in to the humor of the situation. But eventually, we both fell silent again, the energy around us growing contemplative and darker once more. Night began her shift to day, the eastern horizon brightening in the distance. In the living world, birds would be chirping, but there were no birds in the land between the realms of the living and the dead. No animals either, unless they were put there to devour a soul. Like me. That was my reason for being there. That was my job. Devour souls, move them between realms, and feed Death. That was it. I wasn't supposed to care about the living. But I did.

At least, I cared about one of the living.

"I should not have gone to him. I shouldn't have asked Amber's family to reach out to him when we were in Mackinac. I should have just stayed away." I watched the ripples on the lake, enjoying the way the new light of day burned across the tops and sparkled against a still-dark backdrop. Wishing I could be as peaceful and steady. "I brought this threat to his door, and if he dies before his time, it'll be my fault."

"You miss him."

The sharp turn in conversation threw me, Grim's tone making the words a statement and not a question. My brow pulled tight as I had to imagine my entire face screamed *duh* at him. "Of course, but I put him in danger. I brought attention to him."

"Maybe, though—"

Grim never got to finish his sentence because an explosion shattered the silence around us, shaking the earth at the same time. We both jumped to our feet, dual growls joining in the cacophony. Hypnos appeared from the edge of the water, going from smoke to corporeal in barely a step and whipping his cloak around himself in an exaggerated fashion as he moved. Show-off.

"There really was no need to make such a noise," I said, keeping my tone flat. Refusing to give him the attention he so craved. "A simple hello would have worked just as well."

The demon lifted a corner of his mouth to toss us a halfhearted smile. "I prefer to make an entrance."

"What do you want, Hypnos?" Grim asked, looking far meaner than he had been. Seeming much darker and more aggressive, downright ready to brawl.

Hypnos shrugged, exasperatingly lackadaisical. "I was just popping over to see if you'd come across the other Keres sister. I seem to have lost her."

My stomach dropped, every muscle in my body tightening. He had my attention now, and he knew it. "What are you talking about?"

"I was simply wondering if you had any idea where she might be," Hypnos said, still trying way too hard to sound casual. Still failing and allowing the edge of excitement to come across in his tone. "I knew Death had sent her on a mission out this way, but I wasn't sure exactly where or what." He looked up, eyes meeting mine. Lips curling into the smile of a shark. "Or for whom."

I never intended to jump, didn't think about shifting or fighting, but I went from human to wolf in a beat.

Went from flat-footed to racing toward my prey in less than a second. I would destroy that man if he—

"Margaret. Your mate."

Grim's voice sent my paws pounding into the dirt in a new direction. He would take care of Hypnos, as evidenced by the growls coming from behind me. But in that moment, as rageful as that man had made me, I also felt a stronger emotion. A deeper one controlling every one of my actions.

Fear.

If Kapila had Corbin in her clutches, there would be no saving him. Not unless I intervened. She would steal his soul and then hand it over to Death as a snack. She would end the only good thing I had left in this world. I had to save him.

Feeling sluggish and slow on four paws, I shifted forms again, allowing my Keres gifts to take over. Turning into a smoky wraith and taking to the air. I couldn't waste a second. I had to get to the cabin, had to protect Corbin. Had to make sure Kapila didn't destroy the only man I had ever loved.

I had to save him.

I had to hope that Hypnos was wrong.

CHAPTER 5
THE PROMISE

I made it to the little cabin in the woods in mere minutes, flying over the top and surveying the land as best I could. The house appeared empty, the area around it quiet. The day had only barely begun, the world just waking up, but I didn't feel Corbin inside the structure. I doubted he was in there sleeping. No, he was already out. Which meant I had a bigger search to conduct.

I dropped to the ground, landing in my wolf form. I didn't want to yank out all my old memories and feelings, didn't want to open that particular box of pain, but I had to. To save Corbin, I had to put myself through hell.

I was already living in a version of it, so...

With a growl and a moment to focus inward, I pulled up the shattered connection to my mate. We'd once been bonded, been able to feel each other's emotions. Been able to find each other no matter what. That bond had been severed long ago, but the phantom of it lingered. Painful and barely more than a whisper, it remained in place with just enough energy to break my heart and call me across a country when necessary. That echo of what once had been was how I had found him in the first place. It would help me find him again. I hoped.

"By the Fates, please," I whispered to myself, my words reverberating in my wolf's mind. She braced her paws and growled as if preparing. Knowing what was coming. Getting ready for it. And then we worked together to find that broken thread and follow it.

The pain of reconnecting our bond struck us hard, nearly making us fall. Thankfully, my wolf kept her footing after such a hard stumble. As soon as the sharpness evaporated, she took off racing through the woods, adjusting her course as the draw to our mate filled us. Heading exactly where she wanted to go even as the whisper died down and left us with nothing more than a headache that pounded and the briefest whisper of a direction to follow.

Eventually, we found the man in question along the bank of a fast-moving river that likely fed into the lake where I had been hiding. Attracted to the same water I had been looking over. Forever connected.

He appeared to be fishing on an outcropping of rocks,

looking calm and focused. Oblivious to the threat of the black cloud floating above him—the wraith that made up the other Keres sister. Kapila...on the hunt.

I ran faster, but I was still too far away to reach him in time. I knew exactly what the wraith was up to, saw her plan before she made her move, but there was nothing I could do to stop her. One second, Corbin stood on the rocks with his fishing pole in hand and a specter of death over his head. In the next, that specter had dropped down, had enveloped him in her negative energy. Had exerted herself enough to cause him to lose his balance.

Corbin slipped and fell straight into the rough and choppy water.

I kept running, my growl growing louder with every step. The Keres didn't pay me any attention. Instead, she stayed above the bobbing form of my mate. Laughed and played with him—pushing him down then allowing him to resurface. There was no way I would make it to him in time on land, so I shifted again, becoming my own specter of death, and dove straight into the water.

"Fuck," Corbin yelled as he popped above the surface once more. I reached him just at that moment, diving deeper underneath him and doing everything I could to help him stay afloat. Looking up through the mess of bubbles and debris floating in the water, I saw the anger building within my so-called sister. Saw her smoke become darker, more active. More violent. Things would not bode well for Corbin if I only managed to get him out of the water, but that had to be my first priority. Once he was safe, I could deal with her. I would.

I almost looked forward to it.

With a strong force from my inner wolf and a lucky break of a few rocks Corbin practically flung himself against, my mate managed to pull his body from the churning water. I didn't wait for a second to make sure he was okay—instead, I flew straight up into the air, connecting with Kapila just above the waterline. The woman put up a good fight, but I'd been in this form for well over a century. I knew how to utilize my strengths. Teeth gnashing, ooze dripping, I forced her back and up. Never letting her whip around me. Never allowing her even a moment to think about what to do next.

"Your pain is delicious," the woman hissed as we both landed on the riverbank in our human shapes. Thick black fluid dripped from the scratches I'd given her and from the corner of her mouth. I stood whole and hearty, not a single injury. Not even winded. The bitch was mine.

"Your weakness is like candy." I crept forward, letting the inhuman growl of my specter and the one from my inner wolf mingle. Letting them fill the air and sing along with the rushing river. "Do not threaten my mate."

She grinned, the twist of her lips a sick impersonation of happiness. Her overconfidence clear. "He hasn't been your mate for almost a hundred and fifty years. He's nothing to you. Or rather, you're nothing to him."

Oh, but she was wrong. So very wrong. I knew it. Had heard it when he'd called my name. That man still loved me. And I loved him. Always.

"You may think I'm nothing, but I will prove you wrong every time." I stalked closer, growling with every step. Keeping my eyes locked on hers. "You come near him again, and I'll make sure you burn. Or did Hypnos not tell you what happened to the one before you?"

That verbal punch landed exactly as I'd hoped. Her face started to fall but then froze, her body stiffening. She had no idea she was just one more Keres in a long line of them. Same as me, but I had persisted. I had lasted. I would still be standing at the end if she chose to fight me on this. She would be the one crushed into dust.

Luckily for her, the woman chose to keep her afterlife party going.

"I will see you again." She nodded to where Corbin lay on the bank of the river, still breathing hard and looking almost like a man who hadn't made it. Almost, except for the rise and fall of his chest. Except for the shading, albeit lighter than usual, on his cheeks. "Him, too."

There was no ignoring that threat. I jumped at her, letting my wolf come out for just a second before shifting into my specter form. Before going pure smoke and racing through the air right at her. The woman was no dummy—she followed suit and hit the airwaves just as I did. But where I headed straight for her, my intentions clear, she jerked and zagged. She flew as if she had no idea how to drive her new form. Maybe she didn't, but I wouldn't let go of the opportunity.

I swirled around her. Containing her. Forcing her to head only in the direction I wanted her to go. I fought her hard and long, never giving her the chance to find purchase with me. I kept at her until she finally gave up. Until she nearly exploded in a ball of smoky ash and disappeared over the southern horizon.

Until the threat against Corbin had been eliminated... for the moment.

Because I knew—with every fiber of my being—this wasn't over. I'd handed the new Keres an irresistible treat in the form of my pain if she devoured Corbin's soul, and she would come for it again. She'd do it just to show me she had won.

I landed on the rocky shore near Corbin, the weight of fear and grief over my bringing him into this mess making me feel so much heavier than usual. Even my wolf—normally so strong but quiet—whined in my head. Worried. There was no way this could end well.

And poor Corbin. He didn't deserve the attention of so many in the afterlife. He didn't deserve to be hunted by a Keres sister hell-bent on sucking out his soul to please her Death master. He didn't deserve any of this, but I had thrust it upon him.

Even dead, I was the worst possible mate the man could have been saddled with.

I plopped to the earth right beside him, deep in my feelings. Praying to the Fates that they give me a hint of a solution. Some way to know what to do to help Corbin. The world sat silent and still, no signs of life other than the river itself. Always flowing, always moving, always refreshing the flora and fauna. Always a threat to those of us who should have been on dry land.

"Mags."

The whispered word had my head spinning, my eyes zeroing in on Corbin's lips. That had been my nickname once upon a time. What he would call me in the quietest of hours. He would only use that name when we were tangled up together, sweaty and rushing toward some cliff of pleasure, or sated and snuggled close with nothing between us. That word brought up feelings I hadn't even remembered experiencing. And gave me the courage to answer him.

"Corbin?"

He groaned and turned toward me. For the briefest of moments, he opened his eyes, and I would have sworn he could see me. There was no looking through or past—those eyes locked on mine and stopped the breath I technically no longer needed. Froze me into place.

"Mags. I got your message. From Gates—I got it," he said, his eyes going redder. Growing wet. "By the Fates, I have missed you."

My heart broke. Absolutely shattered into a billion pieces within my chest right there on the riverbank. My message. That day on Mackinac Island—the fight that had destroyed the last Keres. I had taken a risk and reached out to the living. The witch who seemed to be able to see me. I had asked that they tell Sandman I was still there. That I loved him. That I missed him.

By the Fates, it had worked. He knew.

I choked out a sob and bent forward, trying to hold myself together. Drowning. I was the one drowning, but not in the river—in my emotions. Pain and loss, fear and grief, bliss and reconnection...hope. So much to feel in such a short amount of time. So many emotions to get dragged down by. I wasn't strong enough to handle them all. All I could do, all I could say, were words of truth and pain.

"I've missed you too. Every single day."

He groaned and closed his eyes, his head lolling to the side. Looking exhausted and likely to lose consciousness once more.

"Stay with me," he said, his words softer than before. Barely more than a whisper. But they galvanized me. Strengthened my resolve and turned me bulletproof.

Stay with him? Death himself could no longer tear us apart.

"Okay."

He coughed, still breathing hard. Still too quiet to sound fully awake and aware. "Promise me."

I gasped, wanting to cry all over again. What he was asking seemed illogical, the dream of a confused and delirious man. A question posed in a way to make the answer impossible. But I knew my answer. I made my vow with a clear understanding that I would likely fail him.

"I promise."

CHAPTER 6
THE PLAN

For days after the almost-drowning, I found myself following Corbin around all the time. I even entered his cabin with him, as intrusive as that seemed. I had to, though. Kapila wouldn't think twice about coming into his home to cause him harm. I had to break his boundaries to protect him and hope he would understand. Though extra time watching him be this new version of himself wasn't a bad benefit. Another gift he started giving me was his words.

"You used to like to put wild flowers in the house," he said one day while out on a walk, talking to me as if he knew I stood on the trail not ten feet behind him. Addressing me for the first time since that day at the riverbank. "I try to remember to pick them, but I miss the smile on your face when you would see them sitting in glasses and jars along the windowsills."

I smiled almost as if on cue when he stopped to pick a single flower from the side of the path, remembering. My sweet, young mate had tried so hard to make me happy. And he had. I'd returned the favor, spoiling him as best I could. We'd had a joyous seventy years to love each other. To find what made the other happy and exploit it every chance we could find. He'd filled my windows with wild flowers, while I had fed him and cared for him and made sure he had everything he needed from me. We'd been truly, utterly, lovingly blissed out.

At least...we were before the fact that our union hadn't yielded a child became a hot button with the pack leadership. Before the day our Alpha decided the childbearing issue must have been Corbin's lacking and called a prerogative to impregnate me himself. Before our entire world had been ripped apart by the claws and teeth of those we'd seen as family. I didn't like to think of those last few days. Thankfully, Corbin kept me distracted.

"You were so young when we met," he said softly, his voice quiet and contemplative. His tone remorseful as he peered down at that single flower. "All long limbs and knobby knees—yet somehow the most beautiful woman I'd ever laid my eyes on."

I chuckled softly, gazing from my spot behind him on

the trail. Unable to take my eyes off the man. "And you had floppy hair and freckles, but my wolf knew in that moment that you were meant to be ours."

We waited in silence for a few moments, him spinning that flower between his fingers and me watching. I enjoyed the quiet time with him. Basking in his energy and pretending to be present *with* him. Perhaps he felt my energy the way I felt his, because he kept talking. Kept sharing those personal moments from so long ago.

"I was so nervous when we began our Klunzad." Corbin shook his head, letting out a single, sarcastic laugh as he slipped the flower behind his ear and began walking again. "But you were quite the seductress."

I rolled my eyes and followed behind him, fighting not to stare at his thick legs as they gobbled up the ground. "We'd been mated for months at that point. We'd already done all the things except that one—of course, I seduced you. If I hadn't, you would have played the 'I'm trying to be respectful' card, and we would have never had sex. Besides, you didn't seem to mind too much."

Corbin continued along the trail, not talking. If I had been alive and this had been an actual conversation, he would have laughed along with me. Would have claimed he had been such an innocent boy. Would have joked more about me being the aggressor in our physical relationship. He would have been right—I *had* been the one to push him. He'd been kind and respectful, and I'd been obsessed with him. When we'd finally had our mating blessed by the Alpha and had hurried off for our Klunzad—a period of time alone, much like a human honeymoon after marriage—I'd been more than ready to join in every way possible with my mate.

My sweet Corbin had been nervous, though. Concerned for me. That first time, that first night together, had become the stuff of legend between us. A point of connection and an affectionate reminder of our past selves. I hadn't thought about it since I'd died. He apparently had.

"I wonder if old Mikaylen ever got over hearing you howling and screaming my name that first night," he said out of the blue as we approached the cabin. "He'd been one of the guards and the only one who'd ever mentioned anything to me."

I huffed, looking toward the horizon as the sun set. Watching as the sky darkened even more in my gray world and remembering a different time. A different place. A different me. "Mikaylen was a bit of a creeper. I'm sure he didn't need to get over anything except being jealous he didn't have the skills to make his mate scream that way."

"Back then, I felt angry that he'd heard you during a time that should have been ours. Still am, I think. But now, I'm prouder than anything. If he'd have tried harder with his bedmates, he could have made them scream, too."

"Exactly."

We returned to his cabin without incident, him walking through the door and me swirling inside in my specter form before settling into the corner. I preferred to stay a shadow inside, just in case, but I enjoyed the quiet moments together when he would talk to me. I truly did.

"Remember that time we spent an entire day exploring the caves on the northern slope of the packlands?" Corbin had moved into the kitchen to place the flower he'd picked in a glass before washing his hands at the sink. "We were so filthy on the way home that we stopped to swim in the creek for a bit, and you freaked out over a snake."

I grinned, remembering. We hadn't been officially mated yet. The Fates had initiated the pull, but we hadn't been blessed by the pack. Hadn't yet had the Rites of Klunzad ceremony. We both knew it was only a matter of time, but there had been rules to follow. Ones I had wanted to break.

"You jumped into my arms," he said as he pulled a bowl out of the refrigerator and opened the lid. "We weren't supposed to be so close, but you did it anyway."

I nodded, fascinated by the smoky tone of his voice. Remembering that moment so vividly.

He grinned, shaking his head as he looked down into the bowl. "By the Fates, but I had wanted to get you naked right then. Say fuck the rules of the pack and lay you down in the grass. If I had known then how things would end..."

Corbin's smile fell, the lightness leaving his handsome face. He turned to put the bowl in some boxy contraption, pressing buttons and making the thing whirr. When it dinged then quieted, he brought his food to the table and set it down on the scarred wooden tabletop, still looking upset. Obviously still angry.

As was I.

Before he took his seat, though, he moved around the table and pulled out the chair opposite him. He did that every night now, pulling out that chair as if to invite me to join him. Not that I ever did, but I liked the ritual. Loved seeing him making a place for me in his life even though I couldn't fill the space.

"If you had known then how things would end..." I said, leading him. Knowing he couldn't hear me but wanting to hear the end of that sentence. Needing it.

Corbin didn't disappoint. "I would have fucked you right then, right there on the bank of that river, then run away with you. I wouldn't have even gone back to grab our stuff." He stabbed his fork into the bowl, twisting and pulling until whatever was inside—some sort of pasta, it seemed—sat on his utensil the way he wanted. "And then I'd still have you with me."

He took a huge bite, the motion far angrier and more aggressive than I would have thought possible. The man seemed furious at the world, at our pack, at our situation. I had been too once upon a time, but the years and the job of being a Keres had worn down some of the rough edges. I felt more sad than mad at that point, but I could understand his emotional state. His ire. I couldn't join him in those emotions.

I stared past him as I wallowed in grief, my dead heart breaking again even all these years later. "No one escapes Death forever."

And so the days passed—me following Corbin around like a puppy, him speaking to me as if he knew I was close and could hear him, and that damn dining room chair pulled out and ready for me to take my seat every night. I never sat in it, never actually joined him at the table, but I listened. I commented when it felt right. I stayed quiet when it didn't. And I allowed my memories of the two of us to escape their mental strongbox and fill me with both peace and grief.

About a week into this new existence, Grim

returned. I had been standing inside the house with Corbin, listening to him hum softly as he cooked his dinner, when I noticed the menacing shadow right outside the open door. Grim had a way of looking as if he were ready to destroy your entire world at any second—how his witch saw past that to love the man, I had no idea because his very presence elicited a fear response in me. Still, I trusted the man. He was, in fact, the only one in the realm between the living and the dead I *could* trust. So, I slipped outside, ready to hear bad news for some reason. Ready to fight for my mate if I had to.

Grim didn't greet me when I joined him on the porch. "What are your plans?"

Easy question, easy answer. "To keep him alive."

"She won't stop coming for him."

I stared off into the woods, expecting to see her shadowy form flying over the trees. Expecting to feel the danger headed my way right in that moment.

"Trust me, I know," I said, refocusing on the man who had the respect to show up and warn me. "What else can I do?"

"I don't know. We don't have a fire witch handy to burn her."

I snorted a laugh, remembering how Amber and her family had destroyed the last Keres sister. The move had been in self-defense, but it had still been rather impressive. Those fire witches were no joke. I needed to befriend one.

"No witches," I said, answering him. "But Corbin has matches."

Grim grunted softly, a sound almost like...approval? "That won't work, sadly."

"I know." I sighed, stepping toward the railing. Needing a bit of fresh air to clear my head. "There has to be a way to stop her."

"Only Death himself could direct her off this obsession."

"And he won't do that."

The man paused as if thinking, as if considering the option. When he grunted low and quiet, I knew he had come to the same conclusion I had.

"No," Grim said, his voice gruff. "Likely not. He enjoys the chaos too much."

I looked out over the forest, the view from the cabin beautiful even in the land of desaturation and death. There was something calming about all those trees surrounding you. Something soothing about how the leaves seemed to almost dance in the air, singing as they rubbed against one another. Gorgeous to look at, relaxing to listen to, and terrifying as it gave an enemy a million places to hide all at the same time.

"How do you deal?" I asked, not looking away from the view. Not turning to face the Grim Reaper behind me.

"With Hypnos and the threats against your witch—how do you handle it?"

He appeared at my side, staring straight ahead. "She's safe while in the Summerlands, so I get a break. When she's here, it's harder, but I make sure to stay aware. And I have backup."

My lips turned up, my small, sad smile unstoppable. "You call me to guard you."

"Yes."

"Is that why you keep showing up here?"

He turned my way, frowning. "What do you mean?"

"Are you here to guard us as some form of payback?"

A nod and a grunt were the only response I received. Yes, Grim came to watch over us because he felt he owed me. And maybe he did, but I wouldn't have called in that debt.

Deep down, I was glad I didn't have to.

I was also glad I had someone out there watching over Corbin and me.

"I can't," I finally said, my voice barely more than a whisper. The fears that refused to let me go squeezing what little life I had left right out of me. "I can't leave his side."

"I know."

"I'm afraid for him."

"I know that too."

I took a deep breath, readying the next three words.

The ones I didn't trust myself to say. The ones that could come back to bite me later. The three most important words I could ever say.

"I need help."

Grim didn't balk, didn't sigh or grumble either. He inched closer, moving until our shoulders touched. Until we stood side by side and connected, both staring out at the forest. Both still and contemplative. Both ready to fight.

It was Grim who broke our silence. "That's why I'm here, sis."

I choked on an inhale, fighting hard to hold back tears. I hadn't even realized how much I'd needed to hear that—how I'd needed to know someone had my back in this fight. Without thinking about it, I shifted a little closer and leaned my head against his shoulder, letting my guard down for the first time in days. Taking a breather without breath. Behind me, I continued to hear Corbin singing softly. The water eventually turned on, the sound a reminder of what we'd been doing. He had finished eating and had begun cleaning up. He would wash the dishes by hand, dry them, and put them away. He would wipe down the table and the counters, making sure everything he'd used was returned to where it belonged for the night. He would tidy up his home before sitting down to relax for the evening.

He would continue to live his life alone while I

watched, the voyeur in his midst. His protector sneaking a peek into his world. The one who had set the danger upon him in the first place.

The one who had no idea how I could possibly keep that man alive for as long as he deserved to live, even with the Grim Reaper himself as my partner.

CHAPTER 7
THE WARNING

Being around Corbin all the time—listening to him speak as if to me when I couldn't respond—had become some sort of gift made up of torture and love and cruelty. A single present encapsulating the very best and very worst emotions. I needed it to never stop.

Thankfully, Corbin kept an almost-constant running commentary, regaling me with stories of us together, of what he'd done after I'd died, of his feelings and plans for the future. He talked *a lot*, giving me glimpses into his life. The life he'd lived mostly without me.

"I started riding motorcycles specifically to join the Feral Breed Motorcycle Club. I'd wanted to be a protector, do some security work, and fight alongside the good guys who were trying to drag packs like our old one into the modern age." He sat on his deck, his feet propped up on the railing, relaxing in the late-afternoon sun. I stood nearby, shaking my head. My Corbin on a motorcycle—in one of those clubs that performed security for the leader of the National Association of the Lycan Brotherhood. I couldn't believe it. Corbin had never been a fighter while I'd been alive, never gone out of his way to be aggressive. Apparently, he'd grown after my death.

"The best thing about the MC world wasn't the work, though. It was the guys. They still call me every day— Rebel, Gates, Beast, others. They seem to take turns checking in on me. I also get calls from this guy named Scab. You would *not* have liked him, let me tell you. He's a thousand times worse than Mikaylen, but at his heart, he's a good guy. Needs a good punch in the face sometimes, but a good guy."

He continued, talking about the men whom he had ridden and fought with, about their mates and children. About how he had become Uncle Sandman so many times over and had found so much joy in the role. I had been smiling at Corbin, absorbing his words and basking in his existence, when I'd felt the air change. When the sky had seemed to darken a touch. I looked up in time to see a black shadow come flying across the grass toward the porch. I was in motion without thought, ready to fight with no plan whatsoever, but the shadow shifted to solid before I even reached the steps.

"Just me," Grim said, taking one glance over my shoulder at Corbin. "Everything okay out here?"

"We're fine. What's going on?" Because Grim didn't look like the usual Grim. He seemed far more furious and filled with rage than his normal angry self, which didn't soothe my nerves in the least. "Tell me."

"Kapila is stirring up shit with Death because of you and your mate. Hypnos is fueling it, too."

Of course they were. "Let them create drama—Death won't stand for it for long."

Grim glanced at Corbin. "No, he won't. But you never know how he'll respond."

That statement held more truth than I cared to admit. Death was a finicky boss. He could get irritated with Kapila and send her away on some sort of soul-collection task or...

I looked back at my mate, a low buzz forming under my skin as he continued to speak words meant for me. As he told me stories I couldn't pay attention to because I knew exactly where Grim's thoughts had gone. Death could take out Kapila for annoying him, he could punish Hypnos for not controlling her, or he could decide to remove the thing creating the friction between his two Keres sisters. And he would see my mate as a thing, not a person or a soul.

The Fates help us all if Death came for Corbin. There was no escape from that, no coming back, no second chances. There was no afterlife when Death truly took you.

"He won't," I said, knowing Grim didn't need me to explain more than that. "He won't."

"You can't know that." Grim moved a little closer, coming to stand beside me at the railing of the porch. Coming to watch the man at the heart of all of this. "You know the only way to truly be together is if he joins you here in the Reversed."

I cocked my head, finding it odd to hear those words from his mouth. They belonged to his witch. "The Reversed?"

He shrugged one huge shoulder. "It's what Amber calls this plane of existence, because the colors seem desaturated and backward."

"I know, but I've never heard *you* say them."

"She's rubbed off on me."

I grunted. I had been dead a long time—well over a century—but I still had vague memories of what the living plane looked like. This world, where death reigned and souls didn't belong, would never seem normal to me. Dangerous and dark, but not normal.

But I could not use his new language choices as a distraction from the true meaning behind his words.

"I don't want him to die," I said, keeping my voice low. "He deserves a full life."

"You've been here a long time, Margaret. He's been

alive far longer than any human. Perhaps his life is already full and he'd really rather spend some time with you."

"No. He could still live so many more years. Wolf shifters are hard to kill." Unless they were ganged up on and left to bleed out. Four-on-one hadn't been an easy fight. Impossible, really. And those women had all known exactly how to end my existence. I had never stood a chance against them. Corbin was different.

Grim sighed and turned, pinning me with his almost-black gaze. "But is his life full if every minute is spent missing you?"

My temper wouldn't allow my tongue to lie still. "Is yours full when all you do is miss Amber?"

His lips twitched, something like a smile forming on his face. "Ah, but you actually make my point. Amber is dead and safe in the Summerlands. I get her in my arms every other month."

"And is that enough for you?"

"It has to be."

Such a simple statement. Too simple. "My Corbin won't live in the same afterlife as your Amber, though. He's not a witch."

"No, he is not. He would have to remain here."

I was already shaking my head before he finished his sentence. "No. I don't want that. He deserves so much better than this."

"Maybe so," Grim said, pushing off the railing and walking toward the steps leading to the ground. "But I have to ask—have you ever given any thought to what it is *you* deserve?"

"What do you mean?"

He shrugged, walking down the stairs. Retreating. "It's not a sin to be selfish, Margaret."

Oh, but it was. And as Grim left, as he slipped into his smoky form and flew into the trees, thoughts of sin and what was deserved began to swim inside my head. I would have done anything for my mate—absolutely anything. Including keeping us in different planes of existence so he could continue to live out his life. *That* was the selfish part—me wanting to see him succeed and be happy.

But deep inside myself, I coveted what I couldn't have. My mate's arms around me. His smile when I walked into a room. The sweet taste of his kiss. I missed all of it and had for so long. I would have given anything —absolutely anything—to be held in his arms once more, even for just a few seconds.

But his life wasn't mine to give. Or to take.

That would have been far too selfish on my part.

And while such things may not have been a sin, they were definitely wrong.

"I fucking miss you, Margaret."

I turned, slow and weary and almost afraid to look at

Corbin. To see him staring back at me. He wasn't, of course, but that fact surprisingly hurt even more. The twisted fear that he'd somehow seen me was replaced by utter sadness for him as I saw his slumped shoulders, his bowed head. The man had become stuck in his memories. Gone a little deeper than planned. He'd reached the painful parts.

I hated this.

"I miss you too, Corbin."

He shook his head and dropped his feet to the deck. Rising and striding to his door as he said, "I'm sort of happy I almost drowned the other day. Whether that vision was truly you or just my brain playing tricks on me from the lack of oxygen, it doesn't matter. I would happily almost die a thousand deaths if it meant seeing you again each time."

I followed him inside, slow and shaky. Remaining in my mostly human form this time because I didn't have the mental capacity to listen to him and shift in that moment. He *had* seen me. I knew it, had known it, had totally accepted it. And yet, hearing him acknowledge the moment brought up something different within me. Made me feel both excited and so very guilty. My mate shouldn't want to die. Not ever. But if it gave him peace...

"It's not a sin," I whispered, the guilt of even thinking such a thing already eating me from the inside out. I watched as Corbin crossed to the kitchen, yanking cabinets open to grab a short glass and a bottle of whiskey. He poured a hefty shot while standing at the counter, making me want to cry as he threw it back. Without a word, he poured a second, drinking it down just as quickly. Numbing his pain with alcohol. I hated it. Hated everything about that moment, but I couldn't leave him. Couldn't let him grieve in private. I stood as sentinel to the man's pain and anguish. Witness to his true suffering.

After the third shot, he headed to the dining room table, jerking one chair away as if setting it up for a dining partner then moving to his. He dropped into his seat then poured a fourth shot. Pointing the top of the bottle at the open seat when he had a good inch of liquor in the glass before him.

"Sit with me, baby."

My entire body went stiff, my world flipping slightly. I was dead. There was no way he could know that I stood in the corner watching him. And yet...he had spoken specifically to me. He'd made a direct demand of me.

There were times when I could admit to being wrong. This was one of them.

"Just for a minute," I whispered before tiptoeing across the room and slipping into the seat. He didn't react, didn't seem to realize I'd joined him, which was both a relief and a bit of a disappointment. He simply tossed back the fourth shot and slammed the glass down, anger darkening his handsome face. Pain staining it.

All because of me.

How could I ever forgive myself for putting that expression on his face?

How could he ever forgive me for making him live through such agony?

CHAPTER 8

THE STORM

A storm rolled through the night after Grim had given me permission to be selfish. The sky, always so dark and smoky to begin with, went black as the trees bent under the power of the wind whipping across the realm. Flashes of bright light lit up the windows every few minutes, and the world rumbled with the deep reverberations of thunder. I tended to avoid storms since I'd died, flying to another place to keep from having to endure them, but I couldn't leave Corbin alone. So, I stayed, and I grew more anxious with every flash of lightning, and I startled with every boom. The weather made me jumpy, but it turned Corbin nostalgic.

"You were always so afraid of storms," he said in a slow, deep voice from somewhere behind me. "You would tremble in my arms and jump every time the thunder rolled across the sky."

I turned away from the windows, finding my mate cleaning up from his quick dinner in the kitchen. Remembering right along with him. I didn't have recollections of the fear, really—though it totally made sense since storms still brought about feelings of anxiety —but I did remember being curled up against him. How warm and safe he'd felt while holding me. The strength I had always found in him when he had wrapped his arms around me and tugged me close.

"I miss you most during storms."

I took a step toward him, unable not to. My poor mate. He looked so sad in that moment, so disconnected and vulnerable. As if my loss hit him harder while the world outside fell victim to Mother Nature. Every crash of thunder seemed to take something out of him, every flash of lightning causing his skin to grow paler. Last night, his drinking had gotten the better of him, made him sad and heartbroken. Tonight, the grief would not be of his own making. The storm would feed it for him.

Just as one of those flashes of lightning struck and the thunder practically exploded over the cabin at the same time, the world went dark. I jumped and whipped into my smoke form, wrapping myself around Corbin in a blink. Keeping my eyes on the room around me and ready to fight off any threat. To cut off the coming attack.

Corbin acted much calmer.

"Power's out," he said casually, not the least bit surprised, it seemed. He turned off the water and wiped his hands on the towel he'd kept over his shoulder. "Likely won't be back on tonight. No sense in avoiding the inevitable."

I relaxed and shifted once again, this time to my human form. Watching as he put his things back where they belonged. As he navigated the dark just fine. Eventually, he strolled toward the rear of the cabin. To where his bedroom sat, dark and empty. I remained alone in the shadowy kitchen, staring after him. Battling with myself over what to do next. Fighting the need of what I wanted to do versus what I knew I should do. Heart versus head.

It was Corbin himself who ended the battle.

"You would have dragged me to bed on a night like this," he said from the hallway, still talking to me as he headed down the hallway. Still wanting my attention. Who was I to deny him? I followed after him, keeping my steps light and tracing my fingers along the wall. Feeling as if I were intruding and yet not. The man was talking to me from his private space—did that not equal an invitation? Was I wrong to enter his bedroom?

"I wish you were here, baby," he said, his voice little more than a whisper. I slipped inside the room without another thought, wishing I could somehow show him I *was* there more than I already had. Wishing there were some way for us to come together just this once. That the power of the storm would gift us a moment of connection.

I doubted we would be so lucky.

"Do you remember how I would distract you?" Corbin asked as he stripped his shirt over his head, dropping his hands to push down his pants afterward. Standing naked before me for the first time in over a century. "Do you remember how I would bite your neck and tease your nipples until you would claw at my back and beg me to fuck you?"

By the Fates, I didn't know what to do. He stood there stark naked, hard and obviously ready. Bringing up *those* memories. Yes, he had distracted me during storms. I'd always hated the noise and the lightning, but my mate had used his body to yank my thoughts away from the outside world. If I had been alive, I'd already have been naked and on the bed. Waiting for him. Needing him. The warmth of his skin blanketing mine, the scent of him enveloping me. He would have consumed my senses, refusing to let the outside world into our little bubble. He would have—

"There's never been anyone else for me. Not once in the one hundred and forty-seven years you've been gone. And there never will be."

I froze, staring as he fell back on the bed. As one big

hand slid down his abdomen to grip himself. Had I been alive, I would have been feeling my pulse in every inch of my body. Would have been breathing harder in anticipation. This man—my fated mate—had been alone for well over a century. Had not taken a pleasure mate to his bed even for a single night. It wasn't my business if he had—being dead took me out of the permission position for such things—but knowing he'd abstained, that he'd missed me *that* much, did something to me. It warmed my dead body from the inside. It revived old instincts and responses that I thought had died right along with me.

Needing so much more than to watch from across the room, I slipped across the space and gently crawled onto the bed. It felt wrong and yet not, intruding but invited all at the same time. Corbin wouldn't mind my moving closer. I knew that for sure, and yet I still felt out of place. But I wanted to see, to pretend like we were once again alone together. To encourage my mate to find the pleasure I wished I could bring him. I wanted to participate in giving him that.

So I crawled onto the bed with him, and I licked my bottom lip. And I surrendered to the need of an unfulfilled mate.

"I'm here," I whispered, inching as close as I could, needing to sense the warmth of his skin even if I couldn't actually feel it. "You're still the most handsome man I've ever seen in my life."

Corbin grunted, his head turning my way on the mattress as if he could hear me. His arm and hand moving over himself with quick strokes. With a groan that made me tremble, he moved his other hand to join the party, slipping between his legs as he spread his knees wider. He always had liked to have his balls tugged when I had been using my hand or mouth on him. Perhaps this was his way of remembering how I would take care of him. Maybe he could pretend it was my hands on his flesh, bringing him to completion. Teasing him to the end. I wished it could be. I truly did.

"I loved watching you come," he said, his voice strained. "It was my favorite thing in the entire world. Your cheeks would get so red and your lips would plump up, then you'd make that little gasp and lock your body around mine. I fucking loved that feeling of being held in place by you. As if you couldn't imagine coming without me inside you."

I couldn't. But in that moment, watching my mate pleasure himself with my memories swirling around us, I wished I could. I wished I knew what to do and how. I hadn't dealt with anything sexual since my death—I had thought our sexual urges died along with our physical bodies. At least until Grim had met his witch and I had watched the man hunt after her like a dog in heat. As I had flown over the woods, keeping guard for the two of them while they'd found moments of bliss in each other.

But as I sat on that mattress in Corbin's little cabin in the woods and witnessed my mate jacking himself off, everything changed. A true, physical response to the scene before me grew. A strong one that warmed every inch of me and made me pulse with a craving for something. Made me need.

"Corbin," I said, moaning slightly as I fell onto the mattress beside him. "I don't know what to do."

"Fuck." He arched and bit his lip, a groan sounding from his throat. "Come with me, baby. I need it. Need to know you're still with me like this. Need to know you'd still want me to fuck you if we could."

Of course I wanted. I wanted so badly that I grew wet and trembled with that desire. And of course, I would have done anything for my mate. Fulfilled whatever need he laid bare for me, so I slipped my hand between my legs and rubbed myself. My moves felt awkward and out of rhythm, my body more stressed than turned on as I clumsily tried to remember how to chase my own pleasure.

At least for the first few minutes.

But as I watched Corbin stroke himself like an expert, I began to follow his beat. To match his movements. I mimicked his every stroke, keeping my thumb pressing where I needed the friction as I slipped my fingers inside. As I spread my legs and brought my knees up, opening myself for more. My skin wasn't warm to the touch, my body no longer alive, but there was a response between my thighs. Sexual arousal in a physical form.

"I'm wet for you," I said, teasing myself more. Rolling even closer to Corbin. "I would do anything to have you inside me right now. To let you feel how hot and wet I am just for you."

Corbin groaned and shifted closer, both of us working ourselves in our own little worlds and yet together. Foreheads only inches apart and his warm breath blowing across my face. Lightning lit up the room, followed closely by a crash of thunder that shook the little cabin, but I no longer cared. I could feel the heat rolling off my mate, could smell the scent of his sweat. I had somehow joined him in that moment, fully immersed in pleasure and him and us. He and I were chasing the same peak, our energies weaving together in that single, magical moment. And when we came, when we both grunted and arched and followed each other over the precipice to the relief our bodies needed, when my body clenched down on my fingers and shook with the release, there was no fear of anything outside of that room. There was only us. Entangled intimately for the first time since my death even though we couldn't touch.

"My love," Corbin whispered, curling his body toward mine. "I miss you so much."

I reached out, unable not to. Wanting so much to be fully corporeal, if only for a moment. Needing to feel him.

"I know. I miss you too. So, so much. I never stopped missing you."

"Margaret." He reached for me, obviously falling asleep but still wanting me. Missing me. I mimicked his move, placing my hand over where his lay. Wanting so badly to hold on to him. Wanting for him to know I was right there with him. To join us.

Wanting what I could never have.

CHAPTER 9

THE UNRAVELING

Morning came as it always did, and that sun shining over the tree line to the east brought about a sense of newness. Made me feel refreshed and ready to take on the world. Corbin seemed to feel much the same. We both sprang out of bed and sang the way through our mornings, him chatting with me as if I were there. As if it were his dinnertime and we were having a meal across from each other. Bringing that little bit of evening intimacy through to the rest of the day.

"Do you remember that time we ran down to New Orleans so you could experience Mardi Gras?"

I laughed, wishing that would have been a memory I could forget. "You mean the time I had a panic attack because of all the people and almost shifted in the middle of Bourbon Street?"

He chuckled, his eyes focused on the pan before him. Busy frying something that smelled amazing as he stood in the kitchen. Cooking his breakfast with a small smile on his handsome face. I turned to gaze out the window, relishing the feeling a new day had brought about. In the joy of having spent the night with my mate.

"You were ready to shift right there," he said as he gave the pan a shake, the noise giving away his actions. "I had to hold on to you so tightly to get you to calm down. As if my arms could somehow cage your wolf."

I nodded, my eyes focusing on the mountains in the distance. My mind back in New Orleans. "You did. You nearly broke my ribs squeezing me, if I remember. But it worked."

"Don't get me wrong, I really liked having you so close to me, especially around all those other people, but the moment felt a little stressful."

The sound of him switching off the burner had me turning around. I watched as he spooned his food onto a plate, the clinking of metal on ceramic holding my attention for far longer than I would have expected. I couldn't tear my eyes away from the food he'd prepared. Just enough for one lonely little plate. When I had been alive, he would have made me breakfast as well. Would have doubled what he cooked to feed both of us. For some reason, seeing only one serving—knowing he had learned to adjust his cooking to feed only himself—tore at me in ways I hadn't expected.

Just one more sign that he didn't have me in his life. Just one more example of how he had moved on in some ways.

"Do you remember?" he asked, reminding me of how he hadn't let go of my memory completely. Not yet. "We were outside that crazy bar right there on Bourbon Street."

Yeah, I remembered. I always remembered.

And so the morning went, the two of us having repeating and stilted one-sided conversations alongside each other. Sometimes the words flowed well, the two of us in sync.

"You would have planted a garden if we'd lived on property like this."

"I would have—lettuce and carrots and beets most likely. At least to start."

"I fucking hated it when you grew beets."

"You did because you felt as if you had to eat them. And you should eat them—they're good for you."

"I know they're good for me, but they taste like dirt. I can't get past that."

Sometimes we didn't quite hit our stride, the sentences making sense on their own but not together.

"I bet you'd like riding on the back of my motorcycle."

"I wouldn't."

"We could take a long day ride up through the mountains, stop for some lunch at a tiny diner, spend a few hours running around the woods, then ride back as the sun sets."

"While some of that sounds lovely, the motorcycle part scares me. That's not for me."

"You'd probably get excited hearing the throttle. It's so loud and powerful. A real growl from a machine."

"No, I probably wouldn't get excited by such noise. I would likely—"

"And the guys would love you. I don't ride with the Breed anymore, but they'd still treat you like family."

"Our last family murdered me—"

"We're still tight, the guys and I. You would fit right in with the other mates."

The hours passed, him talking away to me without knowing I was right there listening and responding, while I tried to hang on to some sort of sanity during the off conversations. Still, I kept the words flowing, kept enjoying my time alone with him even when our conversations didn't quite match up. Sometimes, I let him chat at me without a response, basking in the sound of his voice. In fact, when I stopped speaking and closed my eyes, I could almost pretend we were back in the living realm together. That we had escaped the traitorous pack we'd been brought up in and were living a life, just the two of us. That we would spend days like this—talking, doing chores, maybe running errands—before Corbin would move into the kitchen to cook us a simple dinner. I would sit in the living room and watch him, knowing he would be taking me to bed soon so he could get his hands on me. That after the meal, I would be his dessert. I wanted that. My body ached to feel his once more. If I only wished hard enough, maybe I could—

"This won't work."

Grim's words drifted in from the forest as I sat on the porch watching my mate chop wood, voicing my deepest fear as if he had been inside my brain, had me jumping and spinning toward where he lurked. From where he stood in the shadows, watching us. For how long, I had no idea, but he certainly seemed comfortable. The reaper was a bit of a creeper, it seemed.

"Go away," I said, knowing he wouldn't.

As expected, Grim didn't listen. In fact, he took a step closer, practically absorbing shadows as he left the trees, watching Corbin carefully. Looking unhappy about something. "I don't know what your plan is—"

"I don't either, but I need some time to figure it out. I need to work out how I can be with him without putting him in danger."

Grim sighed, walking up onto the porch without waiting for an invitation. He leaned against the railing, staring hard at me, his shoulders hunched slightly as if in a position of defeat. Grim never showed weakness and definitely would never have been defeated by the likes of me, so his stance caught my attention. His mood setting off alarms in my head.

"What?" I asked, unable not to. "Why are you here, like this?"

"Like what?"

I waved a hand to indicate the overall *him* that had my anxiety notching up. "Like *this*. Since when do you slouch?"

He stood up straight, his brow furrowed. "I don't slouch."

"You do now, apparently."

"Keres—"

"Margaret."

"What?"

"Don't call me Keres like it's my name. It's not—it's my title here. My name is Margaret, and you know that."

Grim stood and stared at me, those dark eyes locked on mine making me feel small and weak. Making me feel as if challenging the man in any way had been a mistake. One I refused to back down from.

Finally, he sighed. "Fine. *Margaret*—"

"Thank you."

"—there is no plan that will keep this man alive and safe, so either you need to walk away from him so we can play a little inter-plane scare tactics and get him to leave, or you need to kill him."

"You don't know that this won't work."

"I do know."

"But how do you know? Why do you think I can't keep him alive and spend my afterlife serving Death as is expected of me? Why are you—"

"Because others have tried, and they've always failed." He shook his head, refocusing on Corbin. "You will fail as well."

I took a deep breath, following Grim's gaze to watch Corbin as he worked. On my mate. On the one the Fates had brought to me and promised would be mine. He hadn't moved on from our love. Not in the almost century and a half of our being apart had he walked away, taken another lover, another mate. The man still talked to me as if I were alive. Needing me. Wanting me. We were meant to be together however the Fates had ordained.

"You're wrong," I said, turning toward Grim, comforted by the swoosh-whack as my mate continued to work, oblivious to the discussion happening right behind him. "Our love is strong enough to survive this."

"I wish you would listen to me."

"And if I said the same about you and your witch? If I told you your little dalliances with her could never last, and one day, you'll have to give her up so she can be reincarnated without you...how would you respond?"

He glared my way, black smoke rising from his body as he disrupted the emotional flatness around us. "Amber and I are not in the same situation."

"So, what you're saying is, you know it won't be forever, but you're going to keep playing with fire until one or both of you gets burned. But that I shouldn't be able to do the same. Am I hearing you right?"

"I'm on your side, Margaret."

"No, you're not. Because you don't understand the power of a Fated mate. You don't know what it's like to be tied together for eternity. Don't tell me you're on my side when you want me to walk away from my only love or kill him, because the latter proves the former is a lie." I shook my head, gaze dropping to the porch floor. A deep, endless sadness growing from within me to smother all the happiness I'd been feeling since last night. "Don't ever lie to me, Grim. And don't try to tell me I can't figure out how to make this work. Death chose me as a Keres sister. He saw something strong and powerful within me. If I can exist in the hellscape and do my duties as a Keres, I can do this. I can keep Corbin safe and live in concert with him. It may not be perfect, but I won't fail at it."

Grim stayed silent a long time, long enough for me to raise my head once more and look right at him. For me to see just how worried the man was. About me or his witch, I wasn't sure, but something was deeply troubling to him. Something he simply wasn't going to talk about.

"I wish you luck, Margaret," he finally said, his voice flat, his black eyes no longer meeting mine. "I'll do what I can to support you, but some things only Death himself can stop."

With that, he disappeared in a plume of dark smoke, fading quickly into the clouds above. Leaving me alone with my thoughts and my fears. With my worries. And with my mate.

"They say this will be hard," I said, uncertainty a burn in my gut that wouldn't go away. "That I'm putting you in danger."

Corbin didn't respond, continuing to chop his seemingly endless supply of wood as some sort of music played in the background. A reminder that as together as I felt, we existed in different places. Different realms of existence. Different—

"Doesn't matter," I said, stopping my own thought spiral. "We will figure this out. Right, Corbin?"

He continued to chop and sing along with his music, which seemed like a positive response to me. At least, I would take it as one.

That night, as we once again lay in his bed, as he again murmured my name while taking himself in hand as I watched, Grim's words came back to haunt me. To steal the tiny moment of joy from me.

Some things only Death himself can stop.

He wasn't wrong—Death ruled our world, so only he

could control the outcome. But what Grim had not taken into account was that I already knew that, and I was making plans for the moment I needed to involve Death. If I had to beg and plead with Death to keep my mate safe, I would do so. I'd already given him my afterlife. I didn't know what else he might want in exchange for my happiness, but I would pay it. Every cent.

Corbin was worth it.

I stayed in Corbin's bed again that night, curled on my side and watching my love sleep. Planning hard and wishing so much for some sort of answer to how we could stay together. Finding nothing, but refusing to give up. I would make this work. I would find a way.

I had to.

CHAPTER 10

THE GUEST

Days flew by, hours upon hours of basking in my time with Corbin and enjoying our one-sided conversations. We spent the waking hours outside—cooking, chopping wood, or simply relaxing in the fresh air. Our nighttimes were often passed in his bed, both of us using our hands to bring ourselves pleasure. Both of us coming without the touch of the other, whispering sweet words to a person who couldn't hear them. A weird sort of parallel existence happening between us.

And while I spent my time in tandem with Corbin, I paid more attention to him than ever, truly learning what it was that made the man happy. The way his smile appeared when his phone rang, the laughter when the male voice on the other end told him something about others he knew. They called him Sandman exclusively—never Corbin—which reminded me of Hypnos and the way he stole souls from the living by putting them to sleep. I doubted that was why Corbin had earned that nickname. Maybe one day he'd tell me that story.

Corbin also really enjoyed music. He rarely let the silence reign, always filling the space around him with whatever he had a taste for at that moment. Some of the harder stuff, the songs with the pounding beat and the loud singer, weren't my style, but the peace on his face as he listened made them palatable. I still preferred when he put on something quieter, something smoother. Either way, the sounds coming out of the speakers all around the cabin always seemed to make him smile. He would hum and sing along, whether the song was something on the classic rock station or the one that claimed to be today's hottest metal, whether the screen on his phone said smooth jazz or upbeat classical. He listened to music of all sorts, the sounds bringing him joy. I loved to see it.

On a particularly beautiful morning, when pounding metal music made the entire cabin seem to shake, a wolf shifter pulled into the drive on a huge motorcycle. I flew to the front window, growling softly, watching his approach. Corbin noticed him as well, grinning and hurrying to turn off the music before heading for the door. The man outside dismounted his bike as I stepped outside, taking off his helmet and giving what could only be thought of as a crooked and very shallow smile as Corbin appeared in the doorway. The man made an unforgettable statement with his bushy beard and the scars running up one side of his face. If I had met him in the living realm, I likely would have been afraid of him, but Corbin was not. He rushed to greet the man, the two bumping fists and hugging while slapping each other on the back in a way that seemed horribly painful to me but neither complained about.

"What are you doing here, man?" Corbin asked, grinning at the other shifter.

The scarred shifter lifted one shoulder in a shrug reminiscent of Grim. "Riding through. Thought I'd stop by and take you up on your offer to go fishing. If you've got the time."

"Nothing but time for my brother," Corbin said to the man who was not his brother. I had known his family—this man wasn't one of them. "Come on, let's go hit the river."

I followed behind—my stomach growing sicker with every move—as they strolled to the shed to grab their supplies. Once poles and waders had been prepared, Corbin rushed inside the cabin, filling a cooler with ice and beer before coming back out. The two men walked into the woods, obviously on their way to the river fishing grounds. The spot Corbin where had already almost died.

This was going to be a long day.

Watching Corbin interact with someone who seemed to mean a lot to him was almost more voyeuristic than lying in his bed witnessing him stroke himself at night. The two men obviously had a long-standing friendship and a deep connection. One I knew nothing about. They called each other Beast and Sandman, told stories of others with unusual names like Gates and Rebel, Phoenix and Scab. The motorcycle club men Corbin had ridden with after my death. My mate had lived an entire life without my involvement or me even being able to watch much, a fact that made me feel oddly disconnected from him in that moment. The sensation growing as the minutes passed. As the terrain changed from forest to riverbank. As the men set themselves up for a day of fishing.

"I don't know how you live out here," the man named Beast said, flicking out a line alongside Corbin. "These woods have a creepy vibe to them."

"You scared of the woods now?"

"Not in the least, but these ones have got an energy about them that is working up my wolf."

"What kind of energy?"

"A bad one. Like I'm being watched." He glanced around, his brow furrowed and his eyes dark. "Hunted."

I sat up, following his gaze and taking in the surrounding area. Focusing my senses on the realm of the dead instead of the living. The Beast man could have felt my presence watching them—that was definitely a possibility— but I doubted I would have given off a hunting vibe to the living. No, if his wolf felt like prey, it was because he was, and I wasn't the one hunting him.

"I've never felt unsafe here," Corbin said, frowning as he pulled in his line to cast again. "The woods remind me of my pack days, being back with my mate. It's soothing to me."

"I can see that. How are you doing with—"

"Speaking of mates. How's Calla? The kids? I need some daddy Beast updates."

By the expression on Beast's face, he caught the forced conversation switch just like I did. It hurt, my mate not wanting to talk about me, but I also understood it. Grief was hard, and the weight of it might have gotten easier to carry as time went on, but it never truly released you from its burden. Talking about me may have brought back the knowledge of the pain he carried, so he avoided the subject. Thankfully, Beast didn't call Corbin out on his avoidance. Something that made me think the man had experience with loss.

"The kids are amazing—they grew up too fast, but Calla and I are enjoying some time to ourselves again now that they're all out of the house. She's with the girls this week, having some female bonding time."

"And Calla—she's doing well?"

"Absolutely. Amazing and happy as ever."

Corbin nodded, his eyes going unfocused as he turned to look upstream. His smile falling. "Good. That's good, man. Make sure you keep it that way. Our mates are such a gift from the Fates."

"You're a gift, Margaret," Grim said, appearing out of nowhere as he had a propensity to do and settling in beside me. "Who's the scarred one?"

"Someone Corbin knew from his motorcycle club days."

Grim grunted, watching Beast with a wary eye. "I think I—"

He never got to finish his sentence. One second, the men were in the river, fishing and chatting and spending time together as friends did. The next, Kapila had bulleted across the sky and hovered above them in her smoky Keres form. Grim and I were up and running for the river within a split second, somehow concocting and acting out a plan without a word. While my instincts screamed at me to go to Corbin, Beast was closer and Grim seemed headed straight for my mate. Putting my faith in the other man, I shifted to my wolf form on instinct and ran straight for the big, bad Beast.

The bearded one stood frozen, back arching and body

bowing as Kapila attempted to steal the soul from his living, breathing form. As she tried to kill the man and steal him away from the living realm and into ours. Thankfully, that wasn't an easy task—especially when the person was a healthy, thriving wolf shifter. Whether Kapila knew the struggle she'd run into or not, she seemed surprised not to be able to just snatch and grab. I took advantage of that surprise and shifted to my Keres form, my wolf still in control of my thoughts. My need to protect Corbin at war with the actions of saving Beast instead. Thankfully, it only took one sharp hit for her to release Beast and fly higher, giving both men a chance to escape her. I just had to keep fighting her off.

While Grim used his powers to help the men find safety on the bank, I battled with Kapila in the sky. Pushing her up and away, refusing to give her even an inch. We weren't well matched—I had been a Keres a long time and knew how to utilize all sides of my being, while she was new and almost clumsy with her powers. She didn't give up easily, though. Didn't surrender quickly.

What she did, though, was break away from me long enough to scream, "I won't stop until I win!"

I didn't bother replying, just kept fighting, kept using every ounce of rage I had to force her away from her quarry. I fought and raged and kept pushing until she gave up. With a scream of disappointment, she flew for the western horizon, disappearing into the distance. I stayed afloat for longer than I needed to, both to calm myself and to make sure she wasn't stupid enough to come back for more. I was ready for her—ready to battle to the true death with her. Ready to find a way to set her on fire and watch her burn just like her predecessor had. I was ready to drain her and send her soul to Death to devour.

Thankfully, she didn't come back.

When I finally dropped down to land and shifted to my human form, Grim jumped in front of me, blocking my path to my mate.

"This has to stop," he said, looking angrier and meaner than usual.

"I am aware."

"So what are you going to do?"

I shook my head, shoving past him. Needing to see my mate. "I have no idea yet."

Corbin sat on the riverbank, wet and breathing hard but appearing okay. Beast lay on his back not too far away from my mate, his shirt torn open and his chest rising and falling with the strength of his almost panting breaths. Awake but definitely affected by what had happened. As I walked closer, wanting to make sure he wasn't injured, something on his chest caught my attention. A spot of color on his skin too bright to be a tattoo. One that shouldn't have been there, shouldn't have been seen in this realm. I approached him slowly, almost afraid to admit what I was about to find. Tensing up as the reality of what my eyes were seeing hit me.

"What is that?"

Grim slipped in behind me, frowning as he caught sight of what had stolen all my attention. There, half in and half under the skin of Beast's chest, lay two red threads. The magic makers around shifters—mostly witches like Grim's girl—tended to think of them as a physical representation of our tie to our mates, but Beast didn't have just one. He had two. The first looked old and damaged, worn through and shredded with dark, burned ends. The second lay bright and full of life, almost on top of the other. Obviously, one connection severed and the other strong. How I imagined Corbin's would be if he ever found another mate to take my place.

That thought punched me square in the gut, and I bowed over at the sudden and immediate pain of it. "Oh no."

"Who is that man?" Grim asked, pure rage in his voice.

I shook my head, wishing I could breathe again. Wishing I could do something to calm the instincts swirling to life within me. "His name is Beast. He's Corbin's friend."

Grim pointed, solely focused on the splotch of red on an otherwise grayed-out body. "That's Amber's mate."

I jerked to standing, my entire body locking into place in surprise. "What?"

"Amber was assigned a mate at birth. At some point, long before they met, he battled with Death and won. It severed their connection." He pointed, indicating the damaged thread. "She has the same broken string as he does, but she doesn't have the bright red one with it."

"That must be his new connection. He found another mate."

"You can have more than one?"

I shrugged, my brain still spinning. "Some do. Even alive, some stronger shifters take two mates. But I've never heard of this. Mates don't break connections."

"They did."

They being Amber and Beast. Which, again, seemed impossible. "How?"

"Death did it."

My mind stuttered then spun, thoughts of Death stepping in to break my connections to Corbin infiltrating my brain. Could he have? Did Corbin spend all this time alone and grief-stricken when he didn't need to? Could Death have severed our connection, freeing both of us to deal with the loss—

"Don't," Grim said, making my runaway mind grind to a halt. "Don't even think about it."

"I'm not."

"You are. Don't go down that path."

"I won't."

But I already had. I'd thought the thoughts. I'd put the very idea out into the universe, which meant I'd given it life. The question became, would Death pick up on it and fulfill what he might think of as a wish even though it was the furthest thing from what I wanted?

Would he sever my connection to Corbin and tear us apart, thinking the freedom was better than the connection?

And was it?

CHAPTER II
THE MESSAGE

Orbin and Beast spent the afternoon and evening at the cabin. Neither spoke about what had happened at the river, though the energy between them seemed off. It felt oddly weighty and filled with worry. Their laughter became less easy and frequent, and their conversations didn't flow as smoothly. They also drank more dark whiskey than a normal, not-almost-dying afternoon required. The two men were shaken, for sure. Not that I could blame them. It wasn't every day a specter of death tried to take your perfectly good soul just to piss off another specter of death. At least, not in their reality.

"The couch pulls out," Corbin said, completely distracting me from the trees I had been peering at since before the sun had set. "It's no trouble."

My mate came through the door and onto the deck, his stride long and sure. His feet bare. He carried a plate of steaks and a set of tongs, heading directly for the grill he seemed to love presiding over. Beast came through the same door a minute later with a couple of jars of spices and two beers.

"Thanks, brother. I appreciate the hospitality."

The two men chatted while Corbin cooked, exchanging words and jokes and seeming to all the world to be totally over what had happened at the river. To have finally shaken off the fear of almost dying. But I knew Corbin, knew the set of his shoulders and every possible tone of his voice. I knew the gravity of what he'd experienced weighed on him. I could feel the tension radiating from his body all the way across the deck. That man wasn't over anything. Still.

"My mate would have loved it here," Corbin said, practically out of the blue. I hadn't been paying as much attention to his words until that point, had been focused on his body language and listening for cracks in his armor. Hearing him speak about me to someone else caught my attention.

"Margaret, right?" Beast asked, moving to lean on the railing as he watched Corbin nod. "Anyone ever call her Peggy?"

I growled, the sound not piercing the veil between the worlds, as Corbin began to laugh.

"People did, but she would tear them apart over it. She hated that nickname."

"You don't talk about her too much."

Corbin's grin faded, his smile slowly disappearing as his brow furrowed. "It never gets easier, you know? If I talk about her, that pain comes right back, just as hot and hard as the day she died. I'm able to hide from it better now, but it doesn't disappear."

If I still would have had a heart, it would have shattered right there on the deck. My poor mate. I took a single step forward, raising my arm as if to reach for him. Needing to soothe the tension I felt from him. "Corbin—"

"I can't imagine losing Calla," Beast said, his eyes going unfocused as he stared off into the woods. His words making me stop and realize that I had no way to interact with them. No way to help. I could only listen as he continued. "I would burn the world down—"

"We all say that, but the truth is, once they're taken from you, you're the one who ends up burned to the ground. Grief is..."

Corbin didn't finish his statement, but I felt the rest of his words. Grief was violent and cruel, heavy and soul-shattering. Grief hunted you like a lion, silent but watching, ready to take you down the second you dropped your guard. To sink its claws into you the moment you chose to live without its weight on your back.

Grief didn't fade—it waited.

"Hey," Beast said, recapturing Corbin's attention. "Tell me a good story about her. What's your favorite memory?"

Corbin exploded into laughter, that frown disappearing behind his sunny smile once more. "I don't know if it's my favorite, but—"

"Whatever made you react like that." Beast grinned, giving Corbin a single nod of approval before raising his beer to his lips, ready to take a sip. "Spill it."

"Fine. We used to camp a lot. It got us away from the rest of the pack to be alone. We'd pack a little bag, head out into the woods, and spend the night under the stars. My Margaret was a brave woman, for sure, but she had some deep fears. One being people."

Beast, having just finished sipping his drink, froze for a second before pulling the bottle away from his face. "You mean...humans?"

"Yeah. We were raised in the pack—we didn't really have contact with the outside world much. Anyone new to her, especially if they weren't a shifter, made her anxious."

He wasn't wrong. I *had* been nervous around new people, which was why I had nearly shifted on Bourbon Street. We'd kept our vacations to smaller towns and less touristy places after that trip, but the camping and the tie to my fear of new people... I had no idea what story he was about to tell.

"Ah. So, what...you two run into a stranger?"

"Worse. An entire group of Boy Scouts earning some sort of survival badge."

Beast's face went blank, his dark eyes pinning Corbin in place. "A group of what?"

"Boys. Young boys—maybe age twelve or so. There must have been fifty of them. And Margaret...well, she liked to be naked in the woods when we were alone."

Beast tried to hide his smile behind his beer, but the beard lifting gave it away. As did the small chuckle he coughed. "So...a group of young men thinking they're alone in the woods comes across a naked female. How'd that go?"

I shook my head, the memory coming back to me. The humiliation burning. "Damn you, Corbin."

"My mate—my beautiful, funny, amazing mate—screamed as if she'd been cornered by a bear and ran away from them in her human form. Just took off at full speed through the trees."

"She didn't," Beast said, his laugh growing fuller, louder. "From children?"

Corbin nodded, poking at the steaks with a huge grin on his face. "Bare-assed naked, running through the woods. It took me forever to catch up with her even in my wolf form. Unfortunately, my mate also ran away from the camp we'd set up and ran right into some pretty nasty poison sumac."

Beast's chuckle had turned into constant, rolling laughter. "Still naked."

"Still naked. Even wolf healing can't make that stuff benign. She had a rash from her ankles to her hips. Every inch of her. All because some little boys came strolling through the woods singing a song about a milk jug."

The two men exploded into laughter as I stood with my arms crossed and what had to be a professional-level pout on my face.

"It's not that funny," I said, my tone petulant even to my own ears. "That rash was really uncomfortable."

Eventually, the men stopped laughing, and Beast asked, "So why do you think that popped up when I asked for your favorite memory of her?"

Corbin calmed, his smile growing softer. Sweeter. "I think...beyond the humor of the situation...that was the catalyst for us to move to a deeper level of intimacy. I had to take care of her, you know? And me dealing with that rash on all her parts was pretty humiliating for her, but I took full advantage of the situation. I learned every inch of her. I hovered over her like an Italian mother over her sick son. We had a good four days alone in the woods with me doing nothing but rubbing anti-itch ointment on her and talking to her, distracting her from how uncomfortable she was. There was an intimacy to it that we wouldn't have gotten any other way."

"Your love grew deeper."

"Yeah." Corbin glanced up at his friend. "You been there?"

Beast nodded, taking a sip of his beer before replying. "Every time after Calla gave birth. She always needed help, you know? Caring for my mate like that—making sure her physical and emotional health were shored up—it tied us tighter together. I would have crawled across the floor to blow dirt out of her path if she'd told me the grains hurt her feet. Those moments were always so precious to me because my mate is strong, as I assume yours was. Them letting their guards down and relying solely on us to take care of them...that's true intimacy."

"Yeah, it is." Corbin stared down at the grill for a long moment. "We couldn't have kids. That's what led to her death."

"Her murder."

Corbin looked up, as did I, both of us completely focused on the visitor.

"She didn't just die," Beast said, keeping his eyes on my mate. "She was murdered."

I darted a look at Corbin, watching as his face hardened. As that reminder pushed ugly memories back to the surface. My long-dead heart broke for him all over again as I watched that lionlike grief sink its claws into him.

"Right. Our own family murdered her. People we loved and respected," he finally said, nodding once before pulling the steaks from the grill. "These are done. Let's head inside."

Beast froze for a second, likely hearing the same strain in Corbin's voice that I did, before following his friend inside. I stayed out, giving the two some privacy. Needing a moment to settle my emotions.

Needing time to pull the claws from my own back before walking into the emotional beehive that was Corbin's cabin.

Late that night, after dinner and cleanup and a raucous game of cards, the men sat on the deck under the night sky drinking that dark whiskey Corbin seemed to love so much. They had been sharing memories again—talking about the men they had ridden with in the club, the bikes that had been built in Beast's garage, and the ones that had been destroyed along the way. The words didn't matter; I simply enjoyed being in the presence of the two men who were obviously friends. The tones of their voices soothed something inside me, their rough laughter bringing a smile to my face. I hovered over the corner of the deck in my Keres form, lulled into a sense of peace by the sounds and softness. Relaxed and calm in that moment.

Beast broke that feeling with a handful of words.

"I saw Aoife and Jameson last week."

I shifted to my human shape immediately, landing on my feet without a sound. Aoife. The necromancer. The woman who could traverse the realms of life and death. The one who had come to me and said she would send a message to Corbin. If my heart had been able to beat, it would have been loud enough for the entire world to hear. My fingers twitched, my eyes locked on the man named Beast as I waited to hear what more he would say.

"Those two still out in Arizona?"

Beast tapped his fingers against his glass, suddenly seeming nervous. "Yeah. He's been working with some of the Desert Riders. You remember that club?"

Corbin hummed. "Shifters but not part of the Feral Breed club. Prez was a man named Chiggy, right?"

"Right. Jameson's running some interference between the club and some threat he doesn't want to talk about." Beast took a sip of his drink, peering down into the glass as he said, "Or rather, Aoife is."

"Aoife...the necromancer?"

"Yeah."

Corbin whistled. "What sort of trouble have they

gotten themselves into to require the help of someone who talks to the dead?"

Beast slammed the rest of his drink, wiping a thumb across the corner of his mouth before reaching into his pocket. I stepped closer, needing to see what he had. What he was about to share. The weight of the moment made me feel uncomfortable in my own body—what was left of it—but I stayed in that form. Too afraid to shift. Afraid to miss something.

"Yeah, so...the Riders aren't the only ones reaching out to Aoife lately." He tugged a rolled-up piece of paper from his pocket. I gasped, having seen that paper once before. Knowing what was written on it. At least my part.

"What's that?" Corbin asked, noticing the paper.

Beast handed the scroll to Corbin, keeping his eyes locked on the other man's. "It's a message from Aoife. Or rather, from your Margaret."

The darkness of the night and the desaturation of the world made seeing colors near impossible, but I could have sworn Corbin's face grew paler. He didn't move, didn't jump to unwrap the paper. He simply sat and stared at the bearded man as if waiting for the punch line. As if the very concept of a note from beyond the grave had shattered his brain and left him unable to comprehend the possibility.

My mate finally shook his head, dropping his gaze to

the paper in his hand in disbelief as he murmured, "I don't..."

"Read it. Don't read it. Do whatever feels right." Beast sighed, frowning. "But know that Aoife traveled into the land of the dead for that. *Specifically* for that."

Corbin tightened his grip on the paper. "How did she know?"

Beast sat back, shaking his head. "The fucking witches, man."

Corbin huffed an angry-sounding laugh. "Shadow's mate or Phoenix's?"

"Technically Shadow's. Along with my first mate."

I broke my stare to look toward Beast, remembering that frayed and damaged red thread on his chest. Remembering the words Grim had said.

That's Amber's mate.

"By the Fates," I whispered, pieces of how we were all connected falling into place. How Grim had become obsessed with a dead witch who turned out to have been mated to my mate's friend. How helping Grim and Amber had brought me back to Corbin. How our threads were tangled and messy but woven together. Stronger in their chaotic connections.

Friendships and family bonds and Fate spanning lifetimes and planes of existence, all converging in this one moment. For us.

Corbin still didn't move to unwrap the paper. He

simply sat, transfixed. His body almost unnaturally stiff. I couldn't tear my eyes away from him. Couldn't move for fear of disturbing the tension.

Beast didn't feel the same way.

"I'm going for a run." He set his glass down on the railing and laid a big hand on Corbin's shoulder. "Take your time, man. I can't imagine how hard this must be. Howl if you need me."

Corbin didn't answer, instead remaining locked in place, staring at the piece of paper in his own hand. Completely frozen. Beast headed off the deck and into the woods, likely stripping and shifting along the way. I paid him no mind. His presence wasn't required—this was Corbin's moment. And mine. Ours.

"You can read it," I whispered, creeping forward with anxious steps. "I don't know if it will help or hurt, but you can read it, my love."

As if he heard me, Corbin sighed and threw back the rest of his drink. A man unfrozen but not happy about it. Slowly, as if afraid the paper might jump out and bite him, he brought his hand up and carefully opened his fingers. Time crawled by, seconds turning into minutes as the man I would do anything to talk to haltingly unrolled the scroll. I peeked over his shoulder, wanting to see the note. My handwriting didn't dance across the page, but my words sang from the unfamiliar script. My grief and love and loneliness and adoration laid bare from beyond the grave. My soul, still tied to his, reaching out for one last moment of connection.

"I love you, Corbin. I always have. And I always will."

He sighed, finally finished opening the scroll. Angling himself in the chair to catch the light shining from beside the door to the cabin. Reading my words for the first time in over a century and a half.

CHAPTER 12

Corbin didn't read the note.

Not that night, not the next morning, not after a loud and almost celebratory breakfast with Beast.

He tucked the note I had dictated for him into his pocket, and he went on with his life.

I didn't think I could be more heartbroken than I already had been, didn't know there was more loss to feel in regard to my mate, but I had been wrong. He didn't read the note, which broke something inside me.

"I'm going to take off this afternoon," Beast said at some point, pulling me from where I had been marinating in my feelings. He had his face buried in his phone, his thumbs bouncing on the screen at lightning speed. "Calla and the girls are on their way back, so it's time to meet them."

Beast tucked his phone away and strode across the living room, looking antsy. Looking like a man ready to hop on his bike right then and get to where he needed to be. Corbin must have noticed the same thing.

"You sure you're up to waiting that long? You look like you're ready to teleport to wherever they are."

"I've missed them," Beast said as he stepped in to wash the dishes Corbin had been scraping and stacking. "Nothing is as bright or as warm as when I have my family around me."

Both men froze for a beat, each likely for different reasons. Beast's words certainly struck a sore spot for Corbin, and Beast probably only then figured out he was punching his friend in a scar that never healed. It was the bearded one who recovered first.

"Did you read the note?"

Corbin's face went stiff, an emotional blankness throwing a cover over the pain that had flashed there. "No."

Beast nodded and washed, his eyes focused on the dishes. He stayed silent for a long time—three plates of washing worth—before he finally asked, "Why not?"

My mate's hand went to his pocket, the one with the note in it. The move was an unconscious thing, almost a tic, but I saw it. Corbin redirected his hand quickly, though. As if shoving off the need to touch that note. Ignoring it.

"I wanted to take my time with it," he finally said. He didn't add more, just grabbed a towel and began drying the dishes Beast washed. Both men stayed silent, the two building a sort of tension between them that left me unable to tear my eyes from the scene before me.

When Beast finished washing the dishes, he wiped down the sink and then moved to the side, resting a hip against a counter on the opposite bank of cabinets and crossing his big arms over his chest. Looking mean and tough and downright scary. A threat, but not to me. To Corbin. My mouth watered, the blackness inside me coming awake at the thought of devouring a soul. If he dared to step toward my mate, if he threatened him in any way, I would destroy him.

I needn't have worried.

"You should read it," Beast said in a voice laced with more concern than I would have expected. "As soon as you're ready, you should read it."

Corbin nodded, his voice quiet as he asked, "Did you?"

"No. I wouldn't have broken trust or inserted myself into your mating like that, man."

Corbin nodded, mumbling something that sounded like okay but not loud enough for me to hear him. Beast must have, though, because he adjusted his stance and speared Corbin with his gaze.

"I did talk to Aoife about the situation when she dropped that paper into my care, though. I wanted to know as much as I could about what I was about to do to you before I agreed to being the messenger."

This time, Corbin's voice came out loud and clear. "What did she say?"

"That the witches got in touch with her and asked for help on your behalf. That your Margaret seemed kind, and that the love she had for you felt just as strong as it would between the living." Beast kept his eyes on Corbin, his beard shifting downward slightly, giving away his frown as he watched my mate seem to collapse forward a bit. His energy of violence quieting as he watched his friend struggle. "But hey...you take your time, okay? There's no rush here. You read it when you think you're ready."

Corbin stood up straighter, nodding. "Yeah, that's the plan. I just...need time to prepare."

All the anger I had at him for not reading the note, that pain his reluctance had caused me—it faded a bit. Corbin hadn't hidden away my words because he didn't want them. He'd avoided them because they caused him even more grief than my not being there. They had reignited the flame of mourning within him, and he'd been trying not to set himself on fire. That knowledge crushed me inside, even though I still wanted him to know my words. Made me feel almost guilty for even agreeing to talk to Aoife.

Beast, meanwhile, seemed determined to keep my mate distracted. "Need me to stick around so you have someone to beat the shit out of when you do? Because I'll volunteer as tribute."

Corbin chuckled darkly. "Nah, but I appreciate the offer."

"It's no problem. I haven't had a good wolf fight with a worthwhile opponent in years." He stretched, his big arms flexing, his chest more of a barrel and larger than a normal man could build. Beast lived up to his name, and I had a feeling he fought just as hard as that moniker implied.

Corbin raised his eyebrows and turned toward his friend, looking slightly devilish. "So you're saying I might have a shot at winning?"

The big man snorted. "Never, but I do like a challenge."

The two laughed, the heavy energy lifting. And just like that, the note seemed to be forgotten by all...except for me. They went about their morning, Corbin pulling out his hunting bows and setting up a target along the driveway. Both men taking turns shooting arrows into hay bales. And all the while, I sat and stewed in an anxiousness that felt too close to dread to ignore it. My mate had a piece of me with him, had my message to him right there at his fingertips. A message that might not be the balm I had intended it to be. A message that could split apart the world Corbin had built for himself.

"You're being overdramatic," I said, trying hard to convince myself that I hadn't just pressed the button on destruction. That I hadn't set into motion the demise of the only man I had ever loved. I finally shifted to my Keres form, flying into the air to watch over the men and the little cabin from a bit of a distance. I needed space to allow my nervousness to subside. I needed a little time away to evaluate the possible outcomes without the constant reminder of my mate's face distracting me.

I needed to know what was going to happen once Corbin read that note, but the timing of his actions was out of my control.

That afternoon, I stayed near the tree line while Corbin and Beast said their goodbyes. Neither man seemed happy to be parting once more, but they each had their own lives to live. And I...well, I had a lot of guilt and fear to deal with. Anxiety, too.

"You can always come back to Michigan," Beast said

as he stood on the gravel driveway, looking up at my mate on the porch.

Corbin shook his head, his hands braced on the porch railing. "This is the place for me to be right now. I can feel it."

Beast didn't look convinced. "What happened yesterday—"

"Was a fluke."

My head spun in Corbin's direction almost of its own volition, my body reacting to the angry tone of his voice. What had happened yesterday—their almost dying in the river—had not been a fluke. It had been a calculated effort to destroy what I loved. Corbin didn't know all of that, but he certainly seemed willing to go to the mattresses to defend their almost-death.

Beast didn't seem ready to blow it off as easily.

"You sure about that?" The scarred one stared for a long moment, his face still and hard. His entire body giving off an energy of disbelief. Of refusal to buy the lie we both knew Corbin had just uttered.

My mate didn't say a thing, which said more than any words could have. The attack at the river had shaken him. It had shaken Grim and me as well, though for very different reasons. Grim would likely spend the next few days at his beloved door to the witch's afterlife—the Summerlands—where he could see the woman he loved. Perhaps she would come through, perhaps not. Either way, he wouldn't be able to stay away from her after meeting her original fated mate. His jealousy wouldn't allow it.

And me...well, I would stay with Corbin and contemplate all the ways my death had affected him. My non-death, really. Perhaps if I had well and truly died, had gone on to whatever afterlife a dead wolf shifter would have experienced, Corbin would have been happier. Perhaps he would have found a new mate. Perhaps...

Perhaps I wouldn't be suffering right alongside him.

As I struggled with the burden my death had caused, the two men said their final goodbyes and parted ways. Beast eventually headed for the main road, leaving behind a quiet and moody Corbin. Not that I blamed him. I felt the same inner turmoil and distress. Felt disconnected and sad. We sat in silence on the porch, looking out over the dark and dreary forest. Both lost in our own thoughts. Both brooding.

Until my mate finally pulled the note from his pocket.

"I guess it's time," he whispered, his voice far softer than I had ever heard it. Filled with a sense of fear I hated hearing from him.

"If you're ready." I floated closer, shifting human and moving to sit beside him. Looking up into his handsome face and wanting to die all over again at the pain I saw there. "Only if you're sure you can handle it."

Corbin shook his head and jumped up, hurrying inside. Before I could push away my shock to react to the move, he returned. In his hands, he held three things— my note, an empty glass, and a bottle of dark whiskey.

His weapons for the evening.

"Better to numb the pain, I think." He poured whiskey into the glass, throwing it back and swallowing it down before refilling it. This time, he took a sip then resettled himself in his chair. He set the bottle down and rested the glass on the arm, still holding on to the note. Focusing on it. "You've never scared me more, Margaret."

I huffed a laugh, wishing he could hear me as I said, "I don't want you scared, my love."

Corbin lifted his glass to his lips and took another sip before using his thumb to begin the unrolling process. When he got to the point where he needed both hands, he set his glass on the chair arm and took a deep breath. His hands shook as he pulled the paper open, a sure sign of his nerves. Of this fear he had over my words. I wanted so badly to soothe him but had no way to do so. Instead, I sat and I watched and I waited.

I knew he had read the first few lines when he grunted and rolled forward, his shoulders practically collapsing.

"My sweet Margaret," he whispered, shaking his head. "Fuck, this is harder than I thought it would be."

"I didn't mean for it to be."

He shook his head and took another deep breath before going silent and still. Before returning his attention to the paper in his hold. He focused on the note, hands still shaking, slowly reading the words on the page. Slowly taking in the message from me sent almost a century and a half after my death.

Slowly unraveling before my very eyes.

CHAPTER 13
THE DEAL

He read the note.

Silent tears falling, breath held throughout, he sat and read the words, his eyes bouncing from left to right and up and down. He must have read that note fifteen times while I sat and watched. While my entire body shook as I remembered some of what I had told Aoife to write down.

Things like how much I had always and would always love him.

Like how I sought him out sometimes to see how he was doing and to bask in his life for a little bit.

How I missed him more with each day instead of less.

I sat while he read, just hoping my simple words were enough to soothe something inside him.

He didn't say a word until the very end, didn't change his position in that chair until he finally dropped his arm and curled over his knees.

"Margaret."

The pain in his voice, the pure agony infused into each syllable of my name, gutted me. I wanted so much to be near him, to be able to ease his pain. But I was in an entirely separate realm from my mate, which meant there was nothing I could do for him.

"I'm so sorry, my love," I whispered, unable to hold it in even though he wouldn't hear my words. "I am so sorry that my death brought you this much pain."

We sat in our shared grief, the night deepening as time moved on without our participation. The winds eventually picked up, a low rumble coming from the west and moving closer. The sky lit up every now and again with bolts of lightning on the other side of the forest. A storm brewing and heading right for us. Life moving on as we stayed stuck in that moment. In that pain. The thunder grew louder, the lightning moving closer, and still, we sat. We mourned. We suffered.

When a light rain began to fall, Corbin finally stood from his chair and moved inside. He didn't make himself dinner, though. Didn't sing or put on music, didn't even light a fire. Instead, he grabbed another bottle of dark whiskey and a glass of ice, plopping into a chair that looked out over the same forest he'd been staring at outside. He sat and he drank, watching as heavy storm clouds rolled through. As the world outside went dark and mean. Violent.

With every flash of lightning, and with every sip of that liquor, Corbin's energy grew threatening, more intense. I could sense the emotional razor's edge he had begun walking along, knew my mate was about to snap. And snap he did, tossing his glass into the empty fireplace and racing outside as the thunder roared and the lightning crashed. Inserting himself into the cacophony of nature at her wickedest.

"It's enough," he screamed into the wind, already soaking wet and looking like a man out of options. "I have had enough."

I stood right behind him, rain falling like tears and running down my face. Knowing his heartache was real. Knowing the pain he had lived through was too heavy for one man to carry. Grief had hit him hard today, and he would find no quick and easy way to relive that burden. Though I would try to help him. I would always try for him.

"I'm here," I whispered, wishing I could hold him. Touch him. Offer my support. "I'm still here."

But Corbin couldn't hear me.

"It's enough," he screamed again, planting his hands

on the railing and leaning forward, the muscles in his arms flexing and the veins popping up. "For fuck's sake, just kill me. Give me death so I can see her again. It's all I want. It's all I've ever wanted."

He choked on that last part, bringing more tears to my own eyes. My poor, broken mate. Why the Fates hadn't severed our connection, why they'd broken Beast and Amber apart but not us, made me rage against them. I loved my mate more than anything in the world, but he was hurting because of his love for me.

The winds blew harder, words and sounds swirling around me. Pressure building as they became clearer, more distinct. I had been wrong—so very wrong—to ever seek out my mate. To ever insert myself into his life. The winds told me all the ways I had messed up, laughing in my ears and pointing out all my failures. Nature had come calling, and her message was loud and clear—Corbin wasn't hurting because of his love for me.

He was hurting *because of me*.

In that moment, with that man breaking down in front of me, I truly understood my part in his misery. I nearly collapsed under the weight of the guilt and pain my actions had brought to us both, nearly stumbled at the push of that truth. And in a moment of pure self-hate, of surrender and wanting my mate to find peace, I whispered the words I had been afraid to voice for well over a hundred years.

"Please release him," I said, nearly choking on the syllables as raindrops streamed down my face. "Break the mating bond so he can find peace."

The sky darkened instantly just before a brilliant flash of lightning exploded across the vast expanse above us. The bolt hit the cabin behind me, a bomb of sound detonating through the night as the porch shook beneath our feet. Corbin jumped and raced down the stairs, turning and looking up at his cabin in horrified surprise. I stayed on the porch, unable to move. Unwilling to fly away from the one thing I knew could end my horrid half-life. Could truly send me to Death. Fire and the dead didn't go together, yet I refused to save myself from the blaze. I luxuriated in it instead.

As the heat warmed my body, I stretched and nearly purred, enjoying the sensation instead of fearing it. I had forgotten how good it felt to not be cold. But as I basked in the warmth, the sky grew even darker, the wind picking up until it seemed a gale had moved in. The chill returned, the fire at my back not receding but moving no closer. For a brief moment, I hoped that I was wrong— that the rain and the wind had already begun to put out the flames. I knew better, though. That wasn't a natural wind. It wasn't a storm or a force of nature. My keeper had answered the call I hadn't realized I'd sent him.

Death had arrived.

Peace left me. That moment of giving in, of surrender,

dissolving into fight-or-flight. Had he been there for me, I would have chosen another option. Would have willingly surrendered and allowed him to end my existence, but I knew that wasn't the case. I hadn't screamed for my own release—I had focused on my mate instead. Which meant Death would do the same.

The only option I had was to fight.

I raced off the porch, screaming into the vortex as a ball of negativity enveloped the area. As Death inched closer. "No. I didn't mean it. Not this way."

The specter made up of nothing more than darkness and endless fear plucked me right off my feet, yanking me up into the air and dissolving my form to the wispy being of a Keres sister. Absorbing me right into his smoky, negative being.

"You should not be playing so much with the living, Keres Margaret."

I flinched at the admonishment, the sound of his voice causing shards of ice to break along my spine and in my mind. "I know. But he's my fated mate, and I couldn't leave him to grieve me so hard all alone."

"You make his grief worse. Your presence feeds it."

That thought tugged on my long-dead heart, making my chest grow heavy and dark with pain. Making the guilt swirl around me like Death himself. "That wasn't my intention."

"I should take his soul for your disobedience."

"No!" I screamed, wishing Corbin had a safe place to go. Wishing I'd never sought him out. "Please. Don't do that. He deserves to live."

"He wants to die."

"He doesn't. He's just confused."

"His mental state is none of your concern. My Keres sisters are not meant to keep people alive. They are servants to me. They feed me with new souls and monitor the land between the living and the dead. You have not been doing your job."

The fear inside me cracked, the anger and guilt creeping out in its place. Making me lose my temper with the one thing in this hellscape that should never be the subject of such emotion. Making me lose my control for just a moment.

A moment that was long enough for me to scream, "I didn't ask for this job!"

Death stilled for just a moment, the darkness practically pulsing around me. I slammed that crack in my control closed fast, snapping my jaws together and pursing my lips. Wishing I could take back the words, the tone. The volume. Death was not one to be disrespected. I knew that, had always known that. Death didn't take to outbursts from the being he had put into place to care for him and his land. Death didn't like disobedience.

I had screwed up.

"Didn't you ask for it?" Death asked, the scrape of his rage-filled voice on my conscience making me whimper in pain. The darkest shadows of him edged closer, the weight of his ire making my very bones hurt. "Are you sure you didn't? Because I clearly remember the day you died, child."

So did I. The pain, the anger, the disbelief that the women I had seen as family for my entire life would do such a thing to me. The absolute rage at the Fates for choosing that ending. The hesitation in the land between. The refusing to let go of my life.

I'd ended up trapped in the land between, a fact that only made my murder that much harder to deal with. That level of hurt and anger never dissipated. Instead, it ate at you. Grew within you. Quietly, slowly, poisoning your mind and body. Seeping into your very bones. That level of pure hatred eventually swallowed you whole.

I was tired of being consumed by it.

"I shouldn't have died at all," I said, unable to control myself. Unable to stop the truth from spilling out as venomous rage pulsed through every inch of my being. All of it directed at the creature before me who had, in my mind, kicked off the past one hundred and forty-seven years of anguish. "I had the perfect life with my mate, and you stole it from me. You allowed Kapila to coordinate my murder when I didn't deserve to die. It wasn't my time, but you let her murder me anyway!"

Death stilled for a moment, the energy around him growing quiet. The wind and pressure easing in an oddly terrifying sort of way.

"Is that the true issue?" he asked, his voice tight and low. Reined in. "You're upset because I brought Kapila here to be your Keres sister?"

In a moment of pure stupidity, I answered him honestly, though not completely. Ignoring all the other reasons my emotions felt out of control. Allowing my hatred for her to cloud my judgment for one second too many.

"Yes!"

Death set me down, his dark energy already dissipating. His intensity lessening as he moved away. "Fine. I'll take care of that issue and then sever your mate's connection to you. Then you should have no problem leaving the living alone. Equal trade."

My dead heart sank, my entire body going stiff as the realization of what I had just done washed over me. As the fact that I had just sold out Corbin in exchange for Kapila's destruction settled into my consciousness.

"No. Please, no. Wait!"

But he was already gone, off to destroy Kapila because I had made a fool's deal with him. Off to upend my world once again and take Corbin away from me for good.

Off to shatter what little sense of normalcy I had managed to scrape together in this hell.

And Death worked fast.

CHAPTER 14

THE DEATH

The death of my mate began quietly.

Grim showed up first, creeping into view from the deepest of the shadows, looking stoic and avoiding eye contact as he hovered near the tree line. Hypnos arrived next, circling Corbin like an animal on the hunt. Grim kept a close eye on Hypnos, grunting softly when the specter moved too close to my mate. Obviously controlling the situation.

I wanted to run to Corbin, to grab him and whisk him away. To find some secret passageway between realms so I could wrap my arms around him. I wanted to keep him safe and alive, but I had more than one problem with that desire. More than one impossible barrier in my way. The first being that I couldn't travel to the land of the living. The second was that, from the moment he had appeared on the grass before the still-burning cabin, Hypnos had put me under his spell. Lethargy had crept over me in an instant, locking me in place, making my inner wolf go sleepy and off-balance. Making her unable to react to that was happening around her. Neither man would risk me shifting to my wolf form and coming after them, so they obviously worked together to quiet my instincts. That was something I had not been prepared for, and the betrayal of it all—the reminder of my own death by people I had trusted—made my throat go tight.

"Please," I choked out, slipping to my knees and fighting just to stay awake. "Don't do this, Grim."

"Death has demanded his price," Hypnos said before he focused on my mate. Grim did nothing, said nothing, and refused to meet my eyes. The man I had considered as close to a friend as was possible in this place had abandoned me. Just as my packmates had all those years ago. Just as I should have known he would, the coward.

Before I could find the resolve to try to reason with them again, Corbin dropped to the ground before me, looking like a man simply too tired to stand any longer. I knew better, though. Hypnos was working his magic, putting my mate to sleep so his soul could be extracted. Killing him in a peaceful, quiet manner—but killing him, nonetheless. Murdering him as I had been murdered. Severing the connection I had been unable to.

I broke, sagging forward as my body surrendered to

the weight of Hypnos's power. Unable to sit up straight any longer, unable to move in any direction but down. The shift in perspective caused the black tears to fall, caused the heart I had long thought was dead to come alive just so it could shatter into a thousand pieces in my hollow chest. I sobbed as the pain of what I was about to witness overtook me, unable to look away and yet horrified to watch. This was it—Corbin would die tonight because of me. Because of my decisions. Because I had not protected him from the beings around me. The guilt of that knowledge was enough to make my dead form dry heave.

The sky darkened suddenly, the wind increasing as the energy around us went still and heavy. As a bubble of negativity encircled us.

Death had arrived for his meal.

"No," I choked out, focusing all my strength into calling Death to me. Needing him to hear my final pleas. "I didn't want this."

"You promised," Death said, his dark energy sucking the last of the joy from my body. His voice causing me to cry out as I finally collapsed to the grassy ground. "To keep you from playing with the living, I have given you what you wanted. Keres Kapila is no longer."

I clawed at the earth below me, fighting exhaustion and sickness as I dug my fingertips into the soil and attempted to pull myself toward Corbin. Doing anything

I could to get to my mate. To save him. Just one more time. "This isn't what I wanted."

"It's what you agreed to, Keres Margaret." Death sent a blast of cold air across the grass, stirring the blades and blowing Corbin down. My mate fell forward, looking decidedly dead already, but I knew that wasn't the case. His soul still resided within his body, a soul Death would never allow to escape him. "Finish this, Hypnos."

But Hypnos couldn't stop staring at me, couldn't stop watching as I sobbed and used my hands to try to drag my body across the ground. As I cried black tears at the pain slicing me apart from the inside. As my world came to an end. He watched me for several long, silent moments. Refusing to move. His face twisted into an expression I had neither the time nor the energy to read. Perhaps he felt horror at watching me try to crawl across the grass. Perhaps he felt anger that I dared to push the limits of his power. Or perhaps he had simply grown bored of me. Whatever he felt, he kept to himself. But he didn't act.

"I cannot, sir," he finally said, stepping away from Corbin and heading for the trees. "I will not destroy two Keres sisters in one night. She doesn't deserve this."

But Death was not one to be disobeyed. "Grim. Take his soul."

Grim still wouldn't make eye contact with me, but I knew. In that moment, I knew I had chosen the wrong partner to work with. Had protected the one who would eventually betray me. I had allowed someone to get close, to learn my secrets, and now he would use that against me.

A low, strangled sound escaped my throat as he took his first step in Corbin's direction.

"I trusted you," I choked out, still unable to move. "*I trusted you.*"

But Grim acted as if he hadn't heard me, never even pausing. He approached Corbin with his hand out. Ready to lead Corbin's soul into his afterlife. Ready to end his mortal life.

And just like that, with one swoop of his arm, Grim severed Corbin's attachment to the world of the living.

"No!" I screamed, finally finding the strength to move...or being released from Hypnos's spell. Either way, I crawled forward, sobbing through the distance. Needing to be next to my mate as he made the transition from living to dead. "Please, no. Please."

"Our deal has been finalized. No more playing with the living, Keres Margaret. Next time, I won't be so kind. Grim, I—"

"Not this one, sir." Grim shook his head, standing between Death and Corbin. "I'll bring you what you desire, but not this soul. Keres Margaret needs to shuttle him to his final resting place to find her closure."

Death growled, the sound low and rumbly. Like

thunder rolling across the sky during a wicked storm. He hovered over us, negativity raining down. The feeling of being watched chilling me as I covered Corbin's dead body with my own. As Grim and I both stood in the way of what Death wanted.

He watched, and he growled, and he made the wind tear through the forest.

"You dare tell me no, Reaper?"

"Just this once." Grim glanced down at me, stone-faced and lacking all emotion. "She brought this upon herself. She should have to finish the job."

His words landed hard, their physical weight punching me in all my sensitive parts. I had brought this on myself. By seeking out Corbin, I had caused the domino effect that had led to his murder. This was all my fault. And I would have to carry his soul through to the afterlife I had been denied as punishment for my sins.

"Fine. I'll do it." Death blew a gust of wind down, the power he sent with it causing Corbin's body to lift. Some sort of magic on the air making the entire realm go absolutely still except for the breath of Death. When he finished, he said simply, "Get rid of what's left."

"Sir," Grim said, looking shocked and almost angry. "You just—"

"Get rid of him, Reaper. I won't say it again." With that, Death dissipated, taking his oppressive negativity with him. Hypnos followed, obviously made uncomfortable by the scene he had witnessed, though not enough to stay and watch me dispose of my love. Only the traitor Grim stayed.

I was not in the mood to deal with him. "Leave us."

"I would, but... His soul won't rise."

"It will, and I will tend to it." I crawled to my knees, black goo still trailing down my face, my entire body shaking with grief and pain and exhaustion, Hypnos's power still draining me. "I will make sure he gets to the afterlife. So, leave. Now."

Grim crouched beside Corbin, a look of regret and compassion on his scarred face. "Death killed him, Margaret. That wind—Death took the soul before I could finish. There is no soul to wait for because Death locked it inside the body. Your mate is lost to us."

I shuddered, falling forward over the dead body of my mate, the emptiness of his passing dragging me down. "You lie."

"I don't, and you know it. You have seen this before." He shook his head, the remorse he had to be feeling clear as day in his dark eyes. "I'm sorry."

But he wasn't sorry. He hadn't severed the connection to his witch. He hadn't given up the only thing that made this dreary, impossible half-life worthwhile. He had stolen something from me...ended a life that could have been continued. Ended everything. He wasn't sorry—he was worried about retaliation.

I couldn't stop the question racing through my brain from slipping out of my mouth. "Why?"

"Why Death, or why me?"

I kept my gaze locked on my mate, the pain a fire burning within me. "Both."

Grim sat silent for a long moment, perhaps waiting for me to look his way. Perhaps collecting his thoughts into some semblance of whatever story he had to tell himself to justify what he'd done. Perhaps just reveling in the pain I continued to exist in.

"Death demanded Corbin's end to punish you."

I scoffed, shaking my head as I wiped the tears from my face. "Isn't this existence punishment enough?"

"Not to Death."

Which was at least accurate. Death had no qualms about what he took. No emotions behind his decisions. He simply swallowed souls without remorse as he had done since the beginning of time itself. If the loss of those souls destroyed the people left behind, that was of no matter to him. He had no interest in the living...or those of us forced to do his bidding. We were just puppets, disposable and good for a while, but nothing necessary. Nothing wanted.

I sighed, unable to look at Grim for a moment longer. Unable to tear my focus away from my dead mate. "And you? Why would you do this? I thought we were some sort of friends."

It took him a long moment to answer. Longer than usual. The silence carried weight, felt charged with some sort of emotion I couldn't place. Felt...off.

"My reasons won't matter today," he finally said, his voice hard. His words final. "Death didn't want you to ever see your living mate again. I followed his directions."

I finally looked up at him, letting all the anger and pain I felt resonate from me. Letting him see what he had done. "And I hate you for it."

Deep down, I hated myself too. Because Grim was right—I wouldn't see my living mate again. Wouldn't see his soul either. Not today, not next week, not in a decade. My mate was gone, no afterlife for him. Just darkness and the great nothingness of a true death. He deserved so much more.

But my mistakes had stolen that from him.

And the devastation of that realization would scar my soul far more than anything else possibly could.

I should have known I couldn't trust the dead.

CHAPTER 15

THE BLOOD

The forest floor beside my dead mate became my home. I refused to move, refused to rise for any reason. My decisions had brought death to the man I would have given my life for, had somehow caused his soul to be lost to any sort of possible afterlife. Me and my selfishness had caused his absolute destruction. There was nothing more important than mourning that.

And mourn, I did. Hours passed, maybe days, perhaps weeks. Time had no meaning to me without Corbin's life sharing some sort of space nearby. I lay in the grass and stared at his body, wishing with everything I had for another chance. Another opportunity. Another moment —just one—to tell him how much I loved him. How much he meant to me. I would have given up my entire existence for him, but that hadn't been an option. So I lay, and I mourned, and I let the rest of the world fall away as if it didn't matter any longer.

Because I didn't matter anymore. Not without him loving me.

Grim came to me after some time had passed, looking concerned and speaking words that no longer made sense. I couldn't be bothered to look his way or even try to listen to him. Saw no reason to pay attention. My world had shattered, and he had been one of the ones swinging the hammer that broke it. I would not find it within myself to forgive him for that. Ever.

Still, Grim persisted in pestering me. He even tried to pull me to my feet at one point, yanking on me as if I were some sort of rag doll on the ground. The joke was on him, though. I didn't resist or push back. I stayed still and pliable, dead weight to him. I didn't even bother to give him a moment of my attention.

He failed in his quest, eventually dropping my limp body back to the earth, albeit a good five feet from where he started. More words came from his mouth, more blah, blah nothingness that I chose not to recognize. That I purposely didn't hear. Words didn't matter in that moment. They never would again.

Eventually, Grim grew weary of my non-response and

disappeared, leaving me alone with my mate once more. I crawled back to Corbin's side and rested, exhausted from all the activity. Grief tearing me apart from the inside out. I was certain that if someone had opened my chest cavity at that point, they would have seen four or five wild creatures with huge claws shredding my internal bits apart. Wild critters with teeth made for destruction, eagerly chomping down on my bones and causing horrific pain and damage. That was the only thing that made sense, the only reason my long-dead heart could possibly hurt so much. Wild little beasties had taken up residence inside me, and I did not have the strength to attempt to evict them. I deserved their torture.

The next time Grim appeared, he had his witch with him. Her long skirt with colors that didn't belong in our realm dragged along the forest floor as she approached, brightening my view for just a moment. Sparking memories of so many happier times. Of Corbin and me alive and camping in the forests around our packlands. Of the flowers he would pick me. The fields filled with them where he would lay me down and make my body his own.

The witch brought color and light and even more pain.

She did not belong in the land of the dead. I liked the woman well enough—she seemed strong, kind, and exceptionally caring when it came to Grim—but nothing she tried to say made sense to me. Words were too hard to understand. My brain had gotten stuck on an endless spiral of every single thing I had ever done that had brought me to this place. To this situation. The visions of my past errors played on a loop, overriding the now and peppered with those joyous moments of the two of us alive and in love. Guilt and grief drowned out any energy needed to understand and left me unwilling to put in the effort to truly hear them. To care enough to try.

The beasties liked when they came, though. Liked the noises and nearness of fresh meat. They became more active, tearing bigger and more painful pieces from my bones. Was that why Grim kept returning? Did he know I was being eaten alive from the inside? Not that I could say I had ever been alive since my death. That didn't even make sense. I didn't make sense. Death didn't make sense. There was no sense to be had.

Grim and his witch didn't say long, both disappearing into the forest. Leaving me with my guilt and my dead mate and the beasties who quieted down in the stillness of the empty forest though never stopped their chomping.

The third time someone appeared, it was Grim and his witch and a familiar woman with the gaze of an owl. The gaze of a death watcher, one of the people who could see through the veils between realms. I had met a few along the way—had been seen a time or two over the past hundred or so years—but only one had crossed through to the land of the dead. One had breached the partition. I couldn't grasp the memory, though. Couldn't remember. Didn't need to, I supposed.

Her presence caused the beasties to go still and the constant pain screaming through my mind to quiet. Restarted my brain in a way nothing else could have. She looked at me, and her expression changed. Mirrored the emotions playing out inside me. It was as if she could see straight into whatever was left of my soul, as if she knew what the beasties had done and how the pain refused to ebb. She saw more than any human should have been able to.

"Help me," I whispered, my eyes burning with unshed tears. Something in those owllike eyes calling to me. My inner wolf awakening from wherever she had been hiding, responding to the woman's presence with a plaintive howl. A call to do something.

And when the woman reached for me, when she held out her hand as if to show it to me, her palm practically glowed red. That may not seem meaningful, but before Grim's witch—whose clothing never quite faded the way the rest of ours did—I hadn't seen true colors since my death. Almost one hundred and fifty years of muted grays and blacks until a witch had come strolling into the realm with colorful clothes. And while the witch's colors had never affected me quite as much as perhaps they should have, that red stood out like a beacon. It called to me, singing my name into the ether. I couldn't look away from it.

"My own wolf shifter mate bleeds for my protection, so I can't stay long."

My memory kick-started, firing up like an old 2-cycle engine left to weather and rot in an abandoned shed. She had come to me. She had brought a message from my mate and had written my words down. She had been responsible for the note Corbin had read the night he died.

She was a necromancer, and her own mate bled to help bring her back from the dead.

My wolf howled again, longer this time. Refusing to back down. Needing me to awaken, to move, to do something. Needing me to act.

Without thought, without a single consideration to the beasties I might disturb, I lifted an arm, needing to feel the red. To know it was real and not a figment of my imagination. The woman moved closer, hand extended and wearing a small smile on her face. Open. Friendly.

Terrifying.

"I'm Aoife, remember? I'm here to help you," she said, pronouncing her name in a way that indicated the Irish spelling and not the more common Eva. That caught even more of my attention and prodded my memories. Yes, Aoife. Necromancer mated to a wolf shifter. She had come to our realm before. It felt like years ago, but perhaps it had only been months. I couldn't remember—time had never mattered to the dead.

The beasties lay dormant inside me, likely waiting to see what this creature would do. I gazed into her eyes, reaching for her hand, still too tired to speak but desperate for that connection. Drawn to it in ways I didn't understand. I finally grew close enough to touch that red spot if I shifted just a bit, staying still for a handful of seconds with my fingers millimeters from her palm. Waiting, worried, but utterly obsessed.

My wolf growled and huffed, giving me the courage to act. The energy to do what I needed to.

I closed the gap between us, my fingers meeting that redness in a moment of pure and utter release. The blood had an instant effect on me, the warm and wet oddly calming. The barest touch of it infused my body with a peace I hadn't known since my death, made the beasties pack up and move out in a single second. Made my long-dead heart thump just once in my scarred and empty chest.

I pressed the full length of my hand against hers, palm to palm. Warm and red and vital to cold and gray and lifeless. Blood of her mate infusing my wolf and what was left of my soul with the most core of energies. I almost shifted right then, almost gave myself over to my wolf form. Instead, I rose to my knees, and I howled to the sky. Still human. More wolf than not. Singing a song of strength through my grief.

"Got her," Aoife said, her words clear and understandable. Her meaning confusing.

I had just made contact, had only just registered the sensations coming through my fingers, when the earth below me began to shake. I broke away from the death seer and curled my body toward Corbin, too afraid to look for the cause. Too worried about losing track of all I had left of him to act. If the earth itself intended to open up and swallow my mate, I would go with him. Would follow him for an eternity.

But the earth didn't open. The ground quieted, the forest returning to the odd silence that reigned in our realm. Everything seemingly back to the normal I so hated. Too silent and still. Unnatural, really. I rolled back over to find that Grim, Amber, and the woman were gone. I was alone with Corbin's dead body once more. I would have thought the past few minutes had been a dream— some sort of fevered fantasy, as impossible as that sounded. I would have totally assumed my brain had manufactured such an interaction. Would have but couldn't.

My palm remained bright red, coated in the warm,

liquid blood of a wolf shifter I had never met. I felt the instinct to protect that liquid, to keep it on my hand and not wash it off. To hold on to the piece of the death seer left with me.

I curled my hand into a fist, placed it on Corbin's chest, and waited for the beasties to return.

CHAPTER 16
THE DOOR

The beasties stayed gone. The shifter blood on my hand stayed liquid and warm. And time... well, time no longer held any relevance for me. At some point, I would need to give Corbin's body to the earth. Knew I would have to get up and move. I wasn't ready yet, but I knew that even in the land between, where the dead moved through to their afterlives or were eaten by Death himself, the forms left behind would eventually rot. I also knew that when the time came for me to leave Corbin's side, to put myself in motion once more, I would head straight for Death. If I begged, perhaps he would destroy my soul. Bring me the mercy I so desired. I didn't need an afterlife, didn't need any sort of reincarnation other spiritualities believed in. I just needed a release from the pain that had overpowered me since the moment Corbin had fallen.

I needed to truly die.

As I contemplated what the peace of nonexistence might look like, I felt the earth below me tremble once more. A flash of light across the forest caught my attention, and I rolled slightly toward it to see. Almost wishing it would be Death himself coming to end me. Still contemplating the end of my existence.

I had a visitor, yes. But it was not Death. Grim had returned.

As the beast of a man stormed toward me, a door appeared behind him. What looked like an old, solid wood slab with slashes and carvings all around it, forming designs that made no sense to my eyes. One I had never actually seen but felt a familiarity with. Felt comfort and warmth from. The door had something like an aura around it, a sense of welcoming. I had to assume that door was the entrance into his witch's afterlife home, the Summerlands. Grim had spoken of it before, had been obsessed with it for a while.

As I watched, Grim's witch appeared at the door, running into the land of the dead with a purpose that took me by surprise. Another woman followed her, one I recognized. One who didn't belong on the other side of that door. Aoife, looking bright and energized and totally focused, raced across the field and headed directly for Corbin's fallen form. Grim stayed behind the two, almost guarding them. Watching over his love with a locked jaw and an energy that screamed deadly.

Why he thought a dead witch and a death speaker—ones he apparently felt it was necessary to protect—were suddenly needed, I had no idea. And I almost had enough energy to want to know. Almost, but not quiet.

"...hurry..."

"...spirit of the earth..."

"...Hypnos..."

Their broken conversation didn't truly hit me, didn't penetrate the grief filling my mind, but something in their actions did. In the way the women hurried and seemed to be working together toward the same goal. In the way the short, blunt comments from Grim punched through the air. I found myself watching, wanting to focus, wanting to know what was going on with them.

"...he could be here...need to start...find his soul..."

Grim looked my way, his words still a mess in my head but beginning to find their path through the haze. His eyes their normal dark and soulless, yet somehow filled with an understanding I hadn't been expecting. What was he up to?

The curiosity I felt seemed to break through the fog around my brain. Instead of dullness, I once again found my senses. Even my wolf sat up and took notice of all the input coming at us. The sound of Amber running around the clearing, her footsteps light and quick. The sight of Aoife closing her eyes and lifting her face to the sky. The scent of a bonfire being set on the other side of Corbin, smoky and slightly acrid. The sense of anticipation these three were building. Something was about to happen. They were going to make sure of it.

As if on cue, the two women threw their arms out and began a chant that, at first, seemed to be in another language. I sat up, watching. Unable not to. Fascinated by their actions. Even Grim, who stood just behind Amber on the other side of the fire, seemed to be whispering the same words.

The energy in the clearing shifted, making my wolf move into protective mode. Making her growl low and deep inside my mind. That energy ebbed and flowed, traveling around the woods in an almost visceral sort of way as we watched and waited. I tracked it, unable not to, determined to understand what was coming.

As I stared, the door creaked open, inviting a warm light into the clearing. The sort that I hadn't seen in so many years. The light of the living coming from a space I knew held the dead. A woman walked through the opening, one with long, dark hair and a face so similar to Amber's I knew she had to be kin. The witch stood in that warm light, practically glowing herself. Brighter and more colorful than even Aoife and Amber. She had an air about her, a power and presence, that fueled my curiosity even more.

I sat up, completely focused on what was happening around me.

The woman joined Amber and Aoife in the clearing, the three joining hands around the fire and chanting words that had only just begun to make sense. Something about home and earth, about mothers and spirits. The ground beneath me began to shimmy as if in response, the entire land of the dead waking up for this moment of magic.

"Air, water, fire, we call upon the earth," the women sang, the woods filling me with an energy I hadn't experienced before. My inner wolf began to howl inside my mind, almost as if being called by her pack. As if something she recognized was coming.

Suddenly, a white mist rose over Corbin's body. There was no mistaking that form as I'd seen them a million times. That was his soul, his life force, a beautiful image of the spiritual base of the man I loved. I choked on a sob as I recognized him, nearly started to cry as the red thread tying us together became more visible. Bright and healthy, the small rope practically burned from within him, glowing and vibrant even in the land of the dead.

Connected across space to me, the red thread looked pristine even after over a century of our being separated. There was something almost glorious about seeing a physical representation of our love for each other. Almost calming.

I was so focused on Corbin, so mesmerized by all I saw, that I missed Grim moving closer. Didn't see him rushing toward my mate's soul until it was too late. With a growl and a hard shoulder press, Grim's body slammed the mist as soon as it became more corporeal and directed Corbin's soul through the open door without stepping over the threshold himself. The glowing woman who had come through that doorway followed right behind him, taking over, and shoving Corbin's soul through the opening. Slamming the door closed behind her. Cutting me off from my mate.

My wolf's howl turned mournful, the hope and joy I had felt at seeing Corbin's soul shattering. The agony born once more.

"No!" I screamed, tears of black falling from my eyes. "Why would you take him from me?"

It was the death speaker—Aoife—who sat before me. Tilting her head to meet my eyes.

"He had one chance for an afterlife, and we gave it to him."

I shook my head, unable to believe what I had just

seen. Unable to rein in the pain that seemed to be trying to devour me. "What do you mean?"

"He didn't want to leave you, Margaret. He was a good mate to the very end, hanging on to your connection even though he couldn't find you in this realm. He deserved better than to slowly dissolve into nothingness here in this place, so we helped him through to his rightful home."

"Where is he?"

Amber approached the two of us, smiling softly. Looking far more relieved than I felt. "He's in the Summerlands with my family. My mother will welcome him home."

I shook my head, unable to understand how that could be better. "But the Summerlands—that's for witches."

The two women looked at each other, some sort of silent conversation passing between them. It was Aoife who finally spoke. "Mostly. It's actually for those who embody the spirit of the corners—fire, water, air, and earth."

I shook my head. "You don't make sense."

Amber settled in beside Aoife, leaning forward as she said, "When I was still alive, I had two sisters. You saw Scarlett—the fire witch. My other sister is Azurine, and she's a water witch. I was born an air witch. Our craft required balance, which meant we always needed to be around earth witches to be able to fully embrace our powers."

Four corners, four legs of a table. That part I could understand in terms of witchcraft. "Okay, but what does that have to do with Corbin?"

"You and your Corbin—you're wolf shifters."

"Right."

"My sisters both mated to shifters. The power of the wolf is an earth energy, so Azurine's wolf-shifter mate, who was the first to join us, brought a balance to us that we had never experienced before."

I sagged, nothing making sense, no matter how I tried to put the pieces together. "I still don't understand."

Amber ducked her head, catching my eyes and smiling softly. "As wolf shifters, your earth energy matches ours. Your kind is allowed to be in the Summerlands, so we sent Corbin's soul there."

Corbin had gone to the Summerlands to...what? Live? Choose reincarnation? I had so many questions, but only one bubbled to the top. "Will he...be like you?"

Able to live a somewhat normal life.

Able to choose to reincarnate.

Able to cross over to the land between where I remained.

Amber glanced at Aoife, her uneasiness showing. "We don't know for sure. Aoife?"

"He's been dead longer than I usually like to work

with," the death witch said, running two fingers over her red palm as if to calm herself. "I hope we weren't too late, but there's no way to know. Previous generations of Weaver witches are working with his soul now to see if they can revive it properly, but there's no guarantee it'll work."

The uncertainty sat heavy on my shoulders, the lack of finality burning through me. "So you threw him into the Summerlands with no idea if he could actually survive there."

Aoife's sharp eyes met mine, her face harsher than before. That owllike expression going from inquisitive to predator in an instant. "It was our only chance to fix the wrong forced upon him, so we took it."

The wrong...that I had caused. She hadn't said it, but I knew. I understood where the blame sat. I fell back, still crying, still mourning. Unsure how to be or what to do next. Unsure if there was a path forward through this. Hoping for Corbin to be given a second life and yet somehow too terrified to think of his soul's rebirth as an option.

"We have to go," Grim said, grabbing me and lifting me into his arms. "We can't stay here to be found."

"But Corbin—"

"Amber will find us if Corbin needs anything."

I glanced over his shoulder to see Amber opening the door and slipping through into the golden light that I'd almost forgotten existed. Aoife was gone as well, both witches returning to wherever they had come from.

Leaving me with the Grim Reaper in the land of the lost souls.

Without my mate.

Still.

CHAPTER 17

THE HOPE

I spent what I had to guess were about three days alone with Grim. Time passed in weird fits and starts in my grief-filled mind, but the man tended to rest at night like a living soul. To stop moving and settle down into a pocket of woods where he went quiet and still. Those rest periods gave me a way to recognize the passing of time around me. That was my point of balance, my touchpoint. Grim resting meant a day had passed.

We helped four souls transition to their afterlives during our days together, Grim hunting them down and leading them to their proper afterlives. I did nothing but follow along, trailing behind the reaper as he shuttled souls out of our realm. I couldn't look at the souls without thinking of the ones they had left behind. Of the mourning happening in the living realm that they would never know about. I hated seeing the dead calm and accepting, heading off to their deserved afterlife, while feeling what the ones left behind had to be feeling. The pain of loss and grief at losing something special. It hit too close to home for me.

Thankfully, Grim handled everything and allowed me to simply exist near him. Never asking me for more than I could give him in terms of attention or focus or...well, anything. In fact, after the first two rest periods, I began to wonder if Grim keeping me close meant he felt the need to babysit me, or if he kept me with him because his witch was too busy and he felt lonely without her. I had a feeling it was a little bit of both.

But my time with Grim wasn't joyous or calming. It wasn't healing in any way. I suffered during those days. Heartbroken and heavy, I trudged through the hours, silently wishing Death could end it all for me. That I could be released from the prison my afterlife had become. Planning for my own second demise once I knew Corbin's fate.

"Stop it," Grim said without warning late on the third day of our trek together.

I frowned but looked up from where I had been staring at the dead leaves on the ground, somewhat surprised by his sudden outburst. "Stop what?"

"Stop moping and wishing Death would come devour your soul."

Guess the whole never allowing me to simply exist thing was over. "How do you know what I'm wishing?"

"I can practically hear your thoughts." He settled deeper against his tree, leaning his head back and looking up into the canopy above us. "You must get past your fear to go on."

I poked at the ground, refocused on those same dead leaves, my head spinning. The grief too heavy to push past or roll out from under. "But what if...I don't want to go on?"

"Why wouldn't you?"

I couldn't answer him, the very thought of voicing my response in a world that Corbin had no part in terrifying. Hurtful. Torturous. I didn't even want to *think* about an endless existence without my mate somewhere nearby. An eternity with nothing to look forward to and the mass of grief slowly burying me until I became a thoughtless Keres, snatching souls and destroying the lives of the living like Corbin's had been destroyed.

I didn't want to think about becoming the villain in anyone's story like Kapila had been in mine.

Grim must have figured out that I wasn't able to vocalize my answer because he grunted, giving me a heads-up before asking his next question. "How did you make it through your afterlife up to this point, Margaret?"

Hearing the man use my name shook me out of the spiral of my thoughts. Gave me enough focus to answer him as honestly as I could.

"I always knew he was out there. I knew I could sneak a look at him along my own journey. He was safe and living his life, so while I missed him horribly, I was able to focus on that."

Grim grunted again, this time with a darker, more antagonistic sort of tone. "Not much of a life."

"What do you mean by that?"

"How much could he have been living when he was missing his mate?" He finally dropped his head, pinning me in place with his dark eyes. The scars on his face throwing shadows along his cheeks as he said, "That's not living—it's existing."

Which seemed...accurate, and yet... "He was happy. He had friends he cared about and had made a life for himself without me in it. He was fine."

Grim lowered his voice, his words hitting harder. More direct and intentional. "He was empty without you."

His answer stunned me, the emotion behind his words punching a hole in my chest. But he didn't know Corbin, hadn't seen him being calm and peaceful after a long day. Grim couldn't possibly have any more idea of

Corbin's emotional state than I had. "How can you think that?"

He stared at me hard, expression shifting as I watched. His emotional state opened like a flower, this creature of Death's design revealing secrets for the first time. The brutal, scary exterior faded, revealing a face filled with an emotion I'd never seen him wear before. One of pain and loneliness, of missing something. One I never wanted to see again.

"A man knows."

And perhaps he did, but a woman did as well. My mate had been happy. Perhaps not as joyous or at peace as when I had been alive, but he'd had friends. He'd been loved. He had seemed happy.

Most of the time.

Before I could reply to Grim, before I could think up even a single word to say back, the entire world began to shake. Branches trembled and leaves fell as the ground vibrated below us. Grim and I jumped to our feet, him looking ready to destroy any threat headed our way. I had a feeling I didn't look as fierce, but I felt just as prepared. My inner wolf growled low and deep in my mind, ready for me to shift. Ready to give her the reins. But that didn't end up being necessary because nothing came our way. Nothing raced through the woods to attack us. Instead, a door appeared.

"Amber," Grim whispered, the word barely audible.

As the ground quieted and the world went still once more, Grim exploded into the motion. The pounding of his feet as he raced toward the door mimicked that of whatever had just occurred, making me tremble in place.

Or perhaps it was the sudden sense of something exciting happening that I felt as that door opened. Of anticipation and elation. Of an almost impossible feeling of hope that filled me. Corbin had gone through that door. He'd been taken into the Summerlands to have his soul healed. Could he...come back?

"No," I whispered, trying hard to tamp down my excitement so I didn't end up disappointed. But still, I crept forward, approaching the door slowly but directly. My wolf whined and paced, sensing my emotions. Wanting the same things I did.

She got her wish.

One second, there was nothing but light shining through that door. The next, a shadow appeared. A big one. Moving fast. Running toward us. In wolf form.

A wolf I recognized.

"Corbin!" I scrambled toward the door, my wolf howling in my head and a terrifying amount of hope exploding throughout my chest. In mid-stride, my mate shifted from wolf to his human form, giving me the opportunity to see his face. His in-full-color face. He stood out like a beacon against the desaturated background, calling to me. I nearly fell over from the joy, nearly collapsed as his bright-blue eyes met mine—actually locked on me. He *saw* me.

"Margaret," he gasped as we crashed together, pulling me into his arms with a tight grip. There was nothing sweet or romantic about our collision, nothing soft about our hold on each other. The man was brutal in his strength, yanking me off my feet and clutching me to him with arms made of steel. Had I been alive, he would have bruised me. Had I not been a wolf shifter, he likely would have knocked me to the ground.

Thankfully, all he did was make me sob his name a hundred times as I held him just as tightly.

"My mate," he whispered, digging his fingers into my flesh as if afraid I might disappear. "I have missed you so much."

And then he choked out a sob that practically ripped me apart. He had missed me. He had been hurting because of my absence. He had suffered without me. I clung to him, wishing I could soothe those years somehow. Wishing I could make it up to him. All the ways I had likely hurt him slamming into me and making me feel as if I no longer deserved him.

But deserved or not, I wouldn't be letting him go.

"We have an hour," Grim said from across the field where the door stood. He had Amber in his arms, the two looking just as happy to be back together as my Corbin and me.

I gave him a nod and rubbed a hand over Corbin's shoulder, not willing to stop touching him just yet. "Grim says we have an hour."

Corbin growled, his wolf obviously still close to the surface. "That's not enough time. It's not nearly enough."

"It's what we have right now."

He pulled back, crushing his lips to mine in a kiss that turned my world upside down. That ignited something inside me even those nights touching myself in his bed couldn't compare to. He set me ablaze with the feel of his tongue against mine and the growing ridge between us.

Corbin's eyes when he pulled back were dark and hooded, making him look right on the edge of control. "I can do a lot in an hour."

"I'm yours, my mate," I said, leaning in to bite his neck. Needing to taste him, feel him, smell him. Wanting to be surrounded by him. "I'm yours. Always and forever."

With a groan and another quick kiss, he strode into the woods with me still attached to him. Carrying me off to a private spot. I glanced back to see Grim holding Amber in much the same way. The big beast of a man gave me a single head nod, a signal that he would be on the lookout as we lost ourselves. He would make sure nothing snuck up on us, just as I had done for him with his witch when they first came together. We had an hour of alone time while under the protection of the Grim Reaper himself.

We needed to make the most of it.

CHAPTER 18

THE CONNECTION

There was something fantastical about being able to touch and feel Corbin again. To smell his scent around me and hear his breath in my ear. I couldn't find my balance with him, couldn't figure out if I was still in some sort of hellish afterlife or if I had truly died and been reunited with my mate. All I knew was he had me in his arms, exactly where I had wanted to be for close to one hundred and fifty years. And I had no intentions of leaving them.

"Corbin," I whispered for what had to be the thousandth time. My mate growled low and deep, finally ending our walk into the woods and moving to lay me down. He hovered over me, staring in what looked like absolute wonder as I smiled. "My handsome mate. Are you okay?"

He huffed and leaned down to press his lips to mine. Softly, gently. A quick kiss that wasn't nearly enough. "I am not even close to okay, but this? Being here with you? This is amazing."

I giggled and tugged him closer, wanting to stare into his eyes but also too clingy to release him. Needing to feel his weight and be wrapped around him even while missing his body heat. A cold Corbin was better than no Corbin.

He kissed me again, this time a bit more rushed. Lasting a little longer. Moaning as he let his body weight fall into me before breaking apart to whisper in my ear.

"How is this even possible?"

My excitement dimmed, my confusion growing and causing anxiety to rise within me.

"I don't know. When Death took you, I thought it was over. I never expected to see you again." I choked on a sob, releasing him just enough so he could rise on his arm to look down at me. To see me. "But then the witches came…"

"The witches." He leaned down to kiss me again, all slow and deep and incendiary to my soul. "They brought me back to you."

"They did."

"Margaret," he said, groaning my name as he began to move. As he rolled his body against mine in subtle movements. "My sweet Margaret. I have missed you every single day."

"I know, my mate. I saw."

"What did you see?"

"I saw you living your life without me. I saw you spending time with your friends." I spread my legs wider, inviting him between them. Moaning in pleasure when he pressed the hard ridge of his erection into me. "I saw you alone, at night, in bed."

"Baby," he groaned, grinding harder against me. "You're killing me."

"We're already dead."

He stopped moving, practically freezing into place before exploding into laughter. I gripped him tight and rolled us over, straddling his hips as we laughed together for the first time in a century and a half. Enjoying the moment of connection and almost normalcy it brought to me.

"By the Fates, have I missed you." He grabbed my thighs and stared up at me, his gaze dark and fiery. His need apparent. "I can't decide if I want to sit here and have you tell me every moment of what's happened to you since you died or if I want to fuck you through the forest floor."

"We only have an hour."

"So, not enough time for either." He smiled up at me, his hands still holding my thighs. His fingers digging deep into my flesh. "Tell me all you can, then. All you've done since...that day. I want to know where my heart has been."

But I was not in the mood to discuss being made a Keres sister. Not in the frame of mind to sully our reunion with tales of hunting down souls and handing them over to Death instead of allowing them to move into their afterlife. I wanted happiness and connection and bliss.

So I leaned over, pressing a kiss to his lips and rolling my hips against his. He groaned, opening wide and trying to drive the moment. Trying to lead. I was too needy, too excited, and wanted to let him, so I grabbed his hands from my thighs and tugged them over his head. Pinning him in place. His wolf responded, the animal's soul shining through when I broke away enough to look down at him. That beast didn't submit to anyone but me, and thankfully he seemed ready to play.

"Let's try the other option instead." I reached between us, tugging down the loose pants he wore. My own robes were easy enough to adjust, so we were clothed and yet not. Covered and yet skin-to-skin where it counted. I held his length and rocked over the tip, preparing both of us for what was to come. Smiling down at my mate as he arched and groaned and looked about ready to jump out of his skin.

"Margaret," he whispered, twisting underneath me

as if to escape. "I've missed you so much. I want everything, not just this."

My sweet mate. I leaned down to plant a soft kiss to his lips before pulling away. "I know, but this is important, too."

Before I could move, before I could bring us together, he growled and jerked up, flipping us around and landing on top of me. He grabbed my hands and pulled them over my head, pinning me in place with ease. Mimicking what I had done to him.

"Fine, but it's been so long since I've tasted you. Let me indulge."

He moved to slide down my body, started to kiss down the length of me on his way to pleasuring me with his mouth, but the second he dropped below my immediate line of sight, my body froze. Panic welled strong and bright beneath the surface, and my hands began to tremble. I stopped him, had to. Tugged him back up and held his face in my shaky hands as we locked eyes.

His concern screamed from his furrowed brow. "What's wr—"

"Don't disappear on me," I whispered, letting all the fear and pain of the past few days settle into my voice. Giving him my vulnerability in that moment. "I can't handle losing you again."

Corbin didn't move, didn't speak, for a few long

seconds. He simply stared at me, absorbing. Coming to grips with what I needed. Finally, he gave me a single head nod before he returned to kissing me.

His lips were the perfect distraction from what had just happened as he snuck a hand between us and lined us up, as he used his fingers to tease me in the best ways. And when he knew I was ready, when I was practically writhing underneath him and begging him for more, he slid inside me and brought us back together for the first time in over a century.

"By the Fates," he whispered, rocking slowly. Sliding deeper with every push. "I have missed everything about you, including this."

"I know. Using my fingers in your bed while you stroked yourself was never enough."

He paused, pushing up on one arm. "You were...doing that? When I was..."

I nodded, smiling at the way he stumbled over his words. "I wanted so badly to feel you touch my body again."

"Fuck, Margaret." He pounded home, pushing deep and pulling out all the way. Moving faster and harder and taking pleasure from me. "I can't... That's so... I just want you, baby. I need you."

"Take me, then."

And he did. He played my body expertly, remembering every trick and tease to bring me pleasure.

My handsome mate loved me physically until we were both spent, left to lie on the forest floor in a tangle of limbs. Until we were so sated and tired, all we could do was cuddle and laugh together.

Until the hour ended and Grim began calling for me.

"We have to go," I whispered, practically shaking in fear. "We need to get you home."

"You are my home, and I'm not leaving you." He tugged me closer, holding me tightly. "I just got you back."

"I know," I said, fighting hard not to let anxiety overtake me. Not to sob uncontrollably and cling to the man who had just been given a second chance. "We'll figure something out."

And we would. I knew it. If we were lucky and he could cross through the door, we could have a life like Amber and Grim—a few weeks apart, a few together in the land between. It would be hard—brutally so—but we'd been lost to each other for one hundred and forty-seven years. We could deal with a handful of days apart.

Maybe.

"Margaret," Grim hollered from behind a stand of trees. "The witches need you both. Come."

Corbin growled as he turned in the direction of Grim's voice.

"Hush," I whispered, running my hand through his

hair until he met my gaze once more. "He's not the enemy."

"He wants us apart. That's an enemy."

"He wants both of us safe." I kissed him one last time, sadness blanketing me as I sighed. "We have to get you back."

"Margaret— "

"We'll work out a plan to see each other, but you don't belong here. You don't deserve to suffer in this realm."

"And you do?"

There was no way to really answer that question. What I deserved had long since been decided. There was no fixing it now.

There was no chance for me.

CHAPTER 19

THE OFFER

We held hands as we headed to where Grim stood with his witch at his side. They weren't alone, though. A woman stood before the doorway, one with long silver hair and an air of wisdom about her. As we approached, she shifted forms, growing younger right before our eyes. Her hair darkening and her skin losing its wrinkles. I stared, gripping Corbin's hand, as my wolf paced in my head. As she made her presence known. She didn't act as if we were in any sort of danger, but something about the woman had her on high alert. I had a feeling Corbin's wolf was reacting much the same way. My mate couldn't tear his eyes away from her.

"Kind Corbin. I have heard much about the wolf who

races through the Summerlands looking for his red thread."

I glanced at my mate, smiling softly when he tugged me closer.

"Should I know who you are?" he asked, his voice respectful but not soft. Guarded.

"Oh, you know. Or rather, your wolves do." She raised her arms, turning her hands palms up almost as if reaching for us. My wolf practically lunged for her but not in fear or rage, in excitement. The beast inside me felt...joyous.

"There they are," she said, smiling our way as she again shifted forms, growing older before our eyes. Middle-aged, it seemed this time. Matronly. "Those creatures who share your soul are quite magical. They're a gift, you see. A gift from a god much older than even I. They are there to protect you, to support you, and to spread magic throughout the world, just as my witches are."

"Our wolves are witches?" I asked, not putting her words together in a way that made sense.

"Oh no, dear. Your wolves are made up of the energy of the earth, much like some of my witches. I also have air witches and fire. Water witches. The four elements are equally represented in our kind, but yours are just the one. A single elemental power gifted to those who understand the privilege of changing forms."

She shifted again, growing older. Returning to the aged woman we had first come upon. Her expression more indulgent and almost sweet. A small smile playing on her wrinkled lips.

"Kind Corbin has been welcomed into the Summerlands, and we invite you back to our safe haven as you await your opportunity to be reborn."

Corbin gripped my hand tighter. "And if I say no?"

The woman cocked her head, looking almost shocked. "Why would you say no, child?"

He glanced at me, pursing his lips before returning his gaze to the woman before us. "This is my mate—the one I have been searching your Summerlands for. We have been forced to spend a lot of time apart since her death, and I do not want to exist another day without her."

My body sagged, my heart breaking. "It's best for you to go with them."

"Not without you." He brought my hand to his lips and kissed the back of it. "I would rather spend an eternity in hell at your side than a single moment in heaven without you."

"Ah, sweet Corbin." The woman chuckled and shook her head slowly as she shifted to her youngest self. "Your red thread is as much of a gift of earth energy as you are, child. The witches of the Summerlands will welcome you both."

Everything went still and silent, no one moving. No one breaking the spell the woman had just cast. I couldn't have heard her correctly.

"Wait," I finally said, unable to make sense of her words. "I'm not like him—I've been dead a long time. I'm a Keres sister. How can I... I can't... What about Death?"

Grim grunted from where he stood to the side, gripping Amber as tightly as Corbin gripped me. "Death won't like her going missing."

The woman straightened, her face dropping into an angry, volatile expression. Her power practically making the air around us vibrate. "Death can deal with me if he doesn't like it. You've suffered enough, child."

Corbin tugged me closer, both of us stepping away just enough to steal what little privacy we could. His energy became an almost visible thing, his excitement pure and unleashed.

"You can come with me," he whispered, his grip on my hand past the point of painful though there was no way I could let him go. "It's nice there—lots of forests and grasslands to explore. But if you don't want to leave here, I'll stay. For you, I'll stay."

I glanced around, taking in the lack of color. The silence of the woods with no other creatures in them. The air of danger the land between always seemed to have about it. My love for my mate wouldn't allow him to give up so much.

"This isn't the place for you."

He lifted my hand to his lips and kissed the back of it. "My place is wherever you are. Something got in the way for a few years, but we're back together. I want us to stay together."

I glanced toward the changing woman, fear and hope and excitement racing through me. I hated hope—it usually disappointed and left me crushed under the weight of failure. But Corbin stood right there, gripping my hand and staring at me just as he had for all our living years together. And his hope practically flowed out of him. I knew he would do it—he would give up the beauty and safety of the Summerlands to stay with me in the land between. He would leave a literal heaven to lie in hell beside me.

I could never ask him to do that.

And I could never walk away from him.

"Okay."

He cocked his head, staring down at me. "Okay what? Do we stay, or do we go?"

"We go. We stay together but go to the Summerlands."

His grin lit up his face, and he leaned down to place a quick but strong kiss to my lips. I relished the contact, wanting more. Needing it. But before we could do that, I needed to walk away from the land between the living and the dead. I needed to leave the place that had been my home for a century and a half. I had to say goodbye.

Corbin led us back the few steps to face the woman—now in her aged, crone form—with his head up and his hand still locked around mine. "She's coming with me."

The woman smiled at me, looking kind and gentle yet thoroughly terrifying in that moment. "You'll be safe in the Summerlands. Safe and protected and joyous. And if you ever choose to reincarnate—"

"No," I said with a shake of my head. "I don't want to reincarnate. I just want to stay with Corbin. Forever."

The woman nodded slowly, changing to her youngest form, the maiden appearing seamlessly right before our eyes. "Then that you will do. But there is one rule."

I froze, my entire body going stiff at the thought of this opportunity being tied to something impossible. At the thought of losing Corbin again and that beautiful ball of hope sitting in my chest being shattered. It would be worse than the beasties, I had to imagine. The pain of hope slicing you apart.

"What is the rule?"

"Once you cross the threshold, you cannot come back. You'll be safe for as long as you choose to remain in the Summerlands." She glanced over her shoulder at the door, a frown marring her pretty face. "Death will not cross over for retaliation if I take you, but I can't protect you if you choose to leave the Summerlands for any reason."

I zeroed in on Grim immediately, noticing the way his witch clung to him. The way they seemed to be made for each other. They were forced to live apart, forced to risk everything to spend time together in Death's realm because he couldn't cross the threshold. I could, but only once.

"Grim..."

"Go," he said, looking mean and fierce and ready to throw me through the door if I even considered pausing. "You've been a good friend, Keres Margaret. But you deserve this chance. Go, take care of my Amber when I can't. Enjoy this gift."

I dropped Corbin's hand and hurried over to Grim, throwing my arms around his neck in the first hug I'd ever offered him. First and last. "Be safe here."

He patted my back awkwardly, obviously not prepared for such affection from me. "I'll be fine."

Corbin tugged on my arm, the innate jealousy of a fated pair obviously springing up. I fell back into his embrace, wanting to cry over leaving Grim alone in the realm. He deserved an afterlife with his witch too, but I couldn't give up my chance with Corbin to stay and help him. I had to be selfish for my mate.

I was allowed to be selfish for me, too.

I looked up at Corbin and smiled, clinging to the hope

igniting within me. Once again holding tight to his hand. "Ready?"

"I was about to ask you that question."

And without a backward glance, we walked through the door to our shared afterlife together.

EPILOGUE

Life in the Summerlands ended up being a gift of endless bounty. The witches embraced Corbin and me fully, coming daily to check in on us and making sure we had everything we could have wanted. They also loved to see the red thread tying us together, commenting on the strength of the braiding and making guesses as to the one who wove it for us. There was no real way to know, but they sure did like to guess.

We were given a little cabin at the edge of the woods with nothing but grasslands before us, the field of green dotted with wild flowers I had never seen before. It took me a handful of days to get used to the riotous colors of the place. It took longer to adjust to the bright sunlight that streamed down every single day. The light wasn't a bad thing per se, but after a century and a half living in a realm with no real color and made up of shadows, the Summerlands felt harsh and uncomfortable.

But Corbin...he felt like home.

"You ready to get up and head to Ximena's?"

I hummed against his chest, my eyes closed against the bright sun, the sound of his voice almost lulling me to sleep. Getting up and heading anywhere wasn't on my agenda at the moment, even though we had plans to spend time with Amber and her mother, Ximena. The get-together had sounded wonderful at the time—I did miss my friend Grim and wanted to find out how he had been doing—but then Corbin and I had taken a run as our wolves. We'd found a small meadow filled with purple flowers and the most perfect section of short grass ever. We'd lain down together under the bright sun...and stayed there. I had no idea how many hours had passed, how long we had simply held each other under the warming rays. Time didn't matter usually.

Today, it did.

"My love," Corbin said, his voice low and deep. Moving out from under me as he said, "We really should go. They're expecting us."

I opened my eyes to find his shining down at me, and my entire body froze for a second. He was so beautiful, so happy and carefree in the Summerlands. I had missed him so much and for so long that it was often hard for me to come to grips with the fact that I had managed to get him back. That we had somehow been blessed with a second chance. That he wasn't going anywhere.

His handsome face, always so very expressive, changed. A frown pulling on his lips and his brow furrowing. "What's wrong?"

"Nothing. Not a single thing."

"Why do you look so sad?"

"I'm not." I reached for him, tugging him into my arms. Wrapping my legs around his when he gave me what I wanted. "I'm not sad at all. I'm just really thankful to spend this time with you."

He hugged me back, rolling his weight onto me. Surrounding me in his touch and scent. "I'm thankful, too. For every second."

"Exactly."

He leaned down to kiss and nip my neck, growling softly in my ear and making me shiver as he whispered, "So, are we standing the ladies up and spending a few more hours out here in the sun?"

I laughed and ran my hands over his back, my happiness overflowing. "No. We should go—they're expecting us. But I'm going to need you tonight."

"You need me every night." He rose to his feet, grinning as he helped me to mine. Tugging me into his arms for a quick kiss before we began the long walk back to the fields where the witches lived.

"I do," I said, gripping his arm a little tighter. "And

I'm thankful to the Fates that I get to have you every night."

He hummed, holding my hand as we reached the tree line. Our walk stayed quiet and comfortable for a good while, both of us more than happy to just *be* together. Eventually, though, the beast inside me woke up and wanted attention. Not the beasties—those were long gone, their pain extinguished by sunshine and love from the man the Fates tied to me. No, my wolf had made the transition with me, and she wanted another chance to run with her mate.

"I think I'm going to shift," I said. Corbin nodded and did the same, both of us in tune enough to go from walking on two legs to running on four without a moment of hesitation. We ran through the forest and out into the grasslands together, not racing but moving faster than a casual run. This had become our life—or not-quite-life. Somehow, we'd been blessed to be able to enjoy our afterlife together, being in love, shifting to our wolves, and spending time running through the Summerlands.

After almost one hundred and fifty years of dealing with death and destruction, it really was a nice change. One I would forever be grateful for.

"There they are," a woman's voice called as we passed into the witch's field where Amber and her mother stayed. Ximena stood on the porch, waving at us. I shifted first, going from fur to skin in a step. Forever grateful that the magic of the place allowed us to shift with our clothing intact. I walked the rest of the way, my Corbin at my side still in wolf form, my fingers dropping to tangle in his fur.

"Come on, love," I whispered as we moved closer. "Time for your human side."

Corbin shifted, grabbing my hand as he rose to his full height. Keeping us connected. "Good evening, Ximena."

"Good evening, my favorite wolves. How was your run through the forest?"

I bit my lip to hold back a grin, trying hard not to think about all the naughtiness we had gotten into out in those woods. Corbin kept a straight face but gripped my hand tighter as if remembering right along with me.

"It was nice," he said, his voice giving nothing away. "We like to get away now and again."

I grinned up at him, holding back a laugh. "The scenery is so pretty out there. Right, my love? All sorts of places to hide and play."

His eyebrow shot up, his smile crooked as if he were still trying to control himself...and failing. "Oh yes. Lots of play happened. Lots and lots."

Ximena's throaty laugh stole our attention. "You two are so filled with sexual energy, you might set my home on fire. Are you sure you wouldn't rather reschedule? I understand if you need a few more hours to yourselves."

I sighed, leaning into Corbin's shoulder. "No, we're fine. We need to spend time with others now and again."

"Well, we would all understand if your time was spent alone as well. A century and a half is a long time to go without the physical love of your red thread." She turned, waving for us to follow her. "Come then. Amber is inside and needs the company."

We walked in together, Corbin holding the door for me. Amber sat at the table across the room, looking distracted and decidedly unhappy.

"Hi, Amber." I walked farther into the space, trying to draw her out. "Rough day?"

She huffed, looking up at me and obviously trying hard to be cordial, her shallow smile not meeting her eyes. "Yes, but that shouldn't reflect on you. It's really nice that you two could come over."

"Oh, kind Corbin. Would you help an old lady out with something?" Ximena shot me a wink, nodding slightly toward her daughter before walking away with my mate. As if that woman needed help with anything. But if she was setting Amber and me up to have time alone, I had to believe there was a reason.

I waited until Ximena and Corbin stepped outside to address the elephant in the room. "Is he okay?"

Amber sighed. "I don't know."

"What do you mean?"

"I haven't been able to see him in a couple of days."

"Is that normal?"

"Not really. Only when he's..."

The look on her face, the fear. I don't know how I knew, but I did. "When he's dealing with Death."

"Yeah."

I stared out the window, memories of my time in the realm between the living and the dead flooding me. Of when Death would call to me for whatever tasks he wanted done. Of how hopeless I always felt. I also remembered how time moved so very differently there.

"When we are with Death," I started, keeping my voice low and quiet, not wanting Corbin to overhear. "Time sometimes slows. His very presence bends it, blurring the lines and causing all sorts of time and space issues. He and Hypnos both."

"Really?" she asked, that dangerous emotion hope in her voice.

"Yeah," I said, hoping my words ended up ringing true. That Grim would show back up at the door whole and hearty. "I wouldn't worry quite yet. Give him time."

She sighed, pasting on a very fake smile. "Okay. I will."

Corbin and Ximena returned to the cottage at that moment, the woman all loud and laughing and shooting me a concerned look. I gave her a smile and nod before focusing on my mate. "Were you able to help, my love?"

"Of course." He came to stand behind me, resting his hands on my shoulders. Sending a chill down my spine at his touch. He must have sensed my response because he held me tighter, growling softly under his breath. "You okay, my love?"

I ran my hand over his, sighing at the contact. "Yeah, just...distracted."

His growl deepened as he dropped down to kiss and subtly bite at my neck. This evening was going to be torture. Pure torture.

"Look at the red threads," Ximena said, smiling our way. "Such a beautiful sight."

"My mate is the beautiful one. I'm just along for the ride." Corbin gave me one final kiss to the cheek before pulling away slightly. "What were you two chatting about in here?"

No sense in pulling any punches, especially with my mate. "Amber's worried about Grim."

Amber gave my husband a tight smile. "I'm sure it's nothing. I just haven't seen his door in a few days."

Corbin frowned. "The one at the end of the porch isn't his?"

Amber froze, her eyes widening. "The what?"

"The door." He pointed to the side as if we could all see through the walls. "There's one at the end—"

He never got to finish his sentence. Amber was up and running before he had the chance.

Ximena just laughed. "I guess I shouldn't blame her. She loves that man."

I caught Corbin's eye, giving him a wink. "I know what that's like."

"You certainly do." Ximena smacked her hands on the counter, grinning at the two of us. "How about we reschedule this for another day? Give Amber and her Reaper a chance to entertain themselves." Her lips lifted into a smirk, and her eyes positively twinkled. "Give yourselves a little extra time alone as well."

I didn't need to be offered such a gift twice. "If you insist."

Ximena laughed, obviously entertained by how quickly I had jumped to my feet. "Go. Both of you. Enjoy each other."

"We'll come by tomorrow," Corbin said, already dragging me out the door. I giggled, knowing we wouldn't be back tomorrow. We likely wouldn't be back for a couple of days. Corbin and I had a habit of getting lost in each other, and I had a feeling we would stay lost for more than a few days.

Or rather, I hoped we would.

"Should we shift, my love?" he asked once we were clear of the porch.

I shook my head, looking over my shoulder at the

door to the land between. At the creepy gray structure that didn't belong in the Summerlands. At where I had come from. The image drew me to it, made me want to feel the chill of the air. Made me miss the desaturated hellscape that had been my home for longer than any other.

"Mags?" Corbin tugged on my arm, making me realize I had taken a step in the wrong direction. I had moved toward the door instead of away from it. Fear filled my chest, and I gripped Corbin's hand tighter.

"I don't know what just happened."

"You looked like you were wanting to go over there." He frowned down at me, obviously concerned. "Were you...wanting to go—"

"No," I interrupted. "No, I just...something about the door." I looked toward it again, unable to shake the feeling of unease it brought to the field. "It calls to me."

"Do you want to go back?"

I spun and looked up at the man who owned my heart. Who was part of my soul. I basked in the glow of his bright-blue stare as the sun warmed my skin and glinted off his light hair. The man was beautiful in full color. He was beautiful no matter what, but Corbin in color? That was a sight I had sorely missed when we were in two different realms. I never wanted to go back to seeing him gray and dull.

So I gripped his hand and tugged him to me, and I

rose onto the balls of my feet so I could reach his lips. And I kissed him with every bit of love and hope and commitment I had in me. He groaned and gripped me tight, hanging on to my hips as he crushed our bodies together. Igniting a fire inside me that never would have burned the same in the land between.

"Baby," he groaned when I bit his bottom lip. "You'd better quit, or I'm going to strip you naked right here."

"I'm not seeing a problem with that."

"Door. Ximena." He kissed me again, not seeming to want to pause any more than I did. Thankfully, his words kept me from losing myself in the moment. Filtered through the fog his touch always caused me.

I pulled away, laughing up at my love. So darn happy and filled with a hope that no longer scared me.

"Race you to our cabin?"

Corbin grinned. "You know I'm going to let you win."

"I know." I stepped back, heading away from the door. Away from my past. Tugging my mate along with me into our future. Together. "But I really like when you chase me."

I laughed and took off running, shifting on the fly. Racing toward the little cabin the witches had gifted us, where Corbin and I could be alone. Where we could spend hours lost in each other.

Where we had all of the after-lifetimes to spend together.

Where we could enjoy the fact that after so much turmoil, we had beaten Death.

For the latest release information, additional content, and promotions, sign up for Ellis Leigh's newsletter.

http://www.ellisleigh.com/newsletter

For new release announcements only, follow Ellis on Bookbub.

http://www.ellisleigh.com/bookbub

About the Author

A storyteller from the time she could talk, Ellis grew up among family legends of hauntings, psychics, and love spanning decades. Those stories didn't always have the happiest of endings, so they inspired her to write about real life, real love, and the difficulties therein. From farmers to werewolves, store clerks to witches—if there's love to be found, she'll write about it. Ellis lives in the Chicago area with her two daughters and a German Shepherd that never leaves her side.

Ellis can also be found writing tropey, erotic shorts with her bestie Brighton Walsh as London Hale, slipping into the contemporary world as Kristin Harte, or taking her signature style into the mystery realm as Millie Thorne.

Let's be social!
www.ellisleigh.com

ellis@ellisleigh.com